TICKET
TO
DEATH

HAUNTED COLLECTION SERIES BOOK 8

Written by Ron Ripley
Edited by Emma Salam

ISBN: 979-8-89476-024-7
Copyright © 2018 by ScareStreet.com

This is a work of fiction. Any resemblance to actual persons, living or dead, or actual events is purely coincidental.

Enter the Realm of Terror...

We'd like to take a moment to thank you for your support and invite you to join our VIP newsletter.

Dive deeper into the darkness with exclusive offers, early access to new releases, and bone-chilling deals when you sign up at www.ScareStreet.com.

Let the nightmares begin...

See you in the shadows,
Scare Street

CHAPTER 1:
A SURPRISE

Nancy Vargas had been away from home for almost a month.

She had traveled down to Texas, then over the border into Mexico, all in an effort to help stem the tide of new tuberculosis cases that had been appearing in the US. Nancy felt her physical exhaustion and mental fatigue more than she cared to admit.

Dropping her keys onto the tray by the door, she flicked on the light and stood still for a moment with her eyes closed. She inhaled the familiar scents of home, enjoyed the sounds of the MacMillan kids as they shouted and played basketball next door, and felt the weight of worry slide off her shoulders.

It's good to be home, she thought. Nancy sat down on the parson's bench against the wall and untied her sneakers, wincing as she did so. Her socks followed, and she pressed both of her bare feet against the cool hardwood of the mudroom. Straightening up, Nancy glanced around and saw a large stack of bundled mail and various packages on the kitchen table, alongside a vase with white and pink roses in it.

Smiling, Nancy stood up and went into the kitchen.

There was a small card balanced against the vase, and she picked it up. Inside, written in Dale's crisp, clean handwriting, was a small note.

> *Hello Beautiful! I took the liberty of getting you some flowers in addition to your mail. I can only assume that your flights were on time and that you did not have to sit beside anyone too horrific. I assume that if you had, I would have heard about it. Give me a call when you feel like having some company!*

Nancy read the card several times, then she leaned forward and breathed in the powerful aroma of the roses. The smell was thoroughly enjoyable and relaxing.

Humming, she put the note back on the table and went to the refrigerator. Inside, she found not only the bottled water that she had put in there four weeks earlier, but a chilled bottle of Riesling white wine, her favorite.

You, sir, she thought to an imaginary Dale as she removed the wine, *are at the very top of the 'good boy' list.*

Nancy poured herself a glass of the fruity white and left the bottle out.

She doubted it would go back into the refrigerator.

More than likely, it'll end up in the recycling bin in an hour or two, she thought, sipping her wine as she walked back to the table. For several minutes, she looked at the large pile of mail and wondered how she, a single woman in her twenties, could accumulate so much correspondence in four weeks.

Sighing, Nancy shook her head and began to sort the mail into three piles. Bills went to the right, personal to the center, and junk to the left.

In the end, the bills and the junk dwarfed the personal, which mainly consisted of a belated birthday card from her aunt and a small, cardboard envelope from someone in Pennsylvania.

After she had gotten rid of the junk mail, Nancy left the bills on the table and carried the bottle of wine, the letter, and the unknown envelope to her family room. Settling down onto her couch, Nancy opened the card first, smiling at the picture of a kitten wearing a birthday hat. She chuckled at the well-wishes her aunt had written inside beneath the printed 'Hoping you have a Cat-tastic Birthday!'

Nancy set the card on the coffee table, so the cat image was facing her, and focused on the unknown letter. She managed to cut through the thick tape with the jagged edge of a fingernail she had broken in San

Antonio, Texas, and extracted the item from inside.

The item turned out to be not one, but two. First, there was a bill of sale that brought a frown to her face, and then an old and yellowed boarding pass for a ship called the *Lady Elgin*.

What in God's name is this? Nancy wondered. *I didn't order anything. Did I?*

Placing the boarding pass on the coffee table beside her birthday card, Nancy looked at the bill of sale and felt her face become hot with embarrassment.

She hadn't purchased anything.

Her neighbor, Mr. Gilbert Bray had.

The mailman had delivered the package to the wrong house.

And I opened it, Nancy thought, sighing. She dropped the bill of sale on the couch, finished her wine, and then refilled the glass. Nancy and the elderly Mr. Bray didn't get along. Mostly because she didn't appreciate the volume at which he listened to his Beatles records. The songs could be heard late into the night up until early in the morning.

And she had complained more than once. Not only to the condo association but to the police as well.

I will never hear the end of this, she frowned. *He won't ever shut up about this one.*

Nancy shook her head, sipped her wine and tried not to think about how the old man would react. After several minutes of sitting in silence, Nancy picked up the boarding pass and examined it closer, thinking, *in for a penny, in for a pound.*

The paper was thick, and ink on it faded with age. Some words, such as the *Lady Elgin*, were still crisp. Others looked as though they were water damaged, and she wondered vaguely what the history behind the piece was.

I'll look it up later, she thought, stifling a yawn. *Now, I think I need a bath. Then, if I'm still awake, I'll see if there are any more episodes of Ghost Hunters on Netflix. Or something on haunted houses. Anything.*

She carried both the wine glass and the bottle to the bathroom, started the water in the tub and proceeded to poke around her collection of bath salts. After a few moments, she shook her head, picked one at random, and dropped it into the water. As the level of water steadily rose, Nancy stripped down and climbed into the almost-too-hot water.

Sinking down into the tub, Nancy closed her eyes and enjoyed the sensation of the water against her skin. She felt the bath salts leach the tensions of the past weeks out of her muscles, and after half an hour, she raised herself up slightly. Nancy added more hot water, then she finished off the bottle of wine. The combination of warmth, exhaustion, and alcohol made her extremely giddy, and more than a little drunk.

And it was for those reasons that she didn't pay much attention to the bathroom lights when they flickered over-head.

She did notice when goosebumps rose along her arms and shoulders, and she shivered as she sank lower in the water. The steam coming off the liquid increased, and her own breath appeared before her as she exhaled. Despite the bath's warmth, Nancy shivered. The light above the vanity mirror flickered and went out, followed a moment later by the recessed lights in the ceiling.

Nancy was alone in a dimly lit room, the only light was provided by a street lamp outside of her guest room window.

For a moment she thought she had lost power, but the street light assured her she had not.

When her home lost power, everyone did. They were all on the same grid. And she knew it wasn't due to a lack of payment, all of her bills were withdrawn automatically each month.

Ignoring the cold, Nancy sat upright and listened.

"It's been a long, long time since I had a bath," a soft voice said morosely.

Fear swarmed over her and Nancy's body shook uncontrollably.

"The lake was so cold," the voice whispered. "Unbearable. Mother tried to save me."

Nancy's eyes darted around the darkness, searching for the source of the voice, looking for a person, for a microphone, *anything*.

All she saw was a glimmer in the doorway, as though the light from the street lamp passed through a thin layer of muslin.

Oh, she thought, *this is just like Ghost Hunters! I can make contact!*

"I didn't know it would be that cold," the voice continued, and Nancy was certain the sound came from the doorway.

"Who are you?" she managed to whisper.

"I'm," the voice hesitated, then let out a shaky laugh. "Isn't that strange? I don't know who I am."

Nancy spoke again, her voice a little stronger. "Where did you come from?"

"Michigan," the unseen speaker said. "Detroit. We were visiting someone. I can't remember who."

"Are you a ghost?" Nancy asked.

"I don't know," the voice said morosely. "I hope not. But I think I am. Yes. Yes, I think I died. That's why I can't find my mother. And why I don't know who I am."

Nancy got a grip on her courage, forced herself speak firmly and asked, "What do you want?"

"I suppose I want to show you what it was like," the stranger said, his tone thoughtful.

"What was?" Nancy asked, then she let out a sharp, terrified shriek as she felt small, cold hands settle upon her head. Her wet hair froze and cracked beneath the ghost's touch, and then the pressure started.

It began slowly and at first, Nancy was able to resist the downward weight.

Within seconds, it was too much, and she tried to twist away.

But the hands remained in place, and the pressure increased.

Nancy felt herself being pushed down towards the water's surface. She grabbed onto the edge of the tub with both hands, but it didn't matter.

"No," she gasped. "Don't!"

"Why?" the ghost asked, pausing.

"I don't want to die!" Nancy shrieked.

"Neither did I," the stranger said and pushed Nancy's head below the water.

CHAPTER 2

A CURIOUS PHONE CALL

The phone rang and disrupted Victor's train of thought. He tried to ignore the call, but by the fourth ring, he gave up. The caller ID listed the number as private and Victor rolled his eyes as he answered it.

"Mr. Daniels," a woman said on the other end.

For a moment he suspected it was Ariana, but while the voice was familiar, it was not Ivan Denisovich's daughter on the other end.

"Who is this?" he asked, leaning back in his chair.

"I'm disappointed," the woman said, chuckling. "This is detective Sara Milton, Mr. Daniels."

"Detective," Victor replied, genuinely happy to hear from her. "This is a pleasant surprise."

"There's the reaction I was looking for," Sara said. "I wish I could say the call is for a pleasant reason."

Victor frowned. "There's not another ghost in Concord, is there?"

"I'm sure there are many," she said. "Just none who are actively killing people. At least none that I know of. Anyway, no, I'm calling because of an issue in Pennsylvania that I need help with."

"Sure," Victor said, straightening up and taking a notepad off his desk, "what can I help you with?"

"I have a friend whose daughter passed away," Sara said, "and I was wondering if you could look into it."

"What happened?" Victor asked, jotting down notes.

"The daughter, Nancy, returned home from an extended trip to the southern border down in Texas. Her boyfriend checked on her the next day and found her dead in the bathroom," Sara said.

"Suicide?" Victor asked.

"No," the detective replied. "They say she was drowned. The medical examiner's report is the reason why I called you. There was frostbite on the top of her head, so much so that her hair had broken off at the scalp. In addition to that, when I spoke with the investigating officer, there's no sign of forced entry. No evidence that anyone was in that house other than her."

Victor circled the word frostbite several times and then said, "How far away is this?"

"Not too far," Sara answered. "She lived in a little suburb of Pittsburgh called Green Tree. From what I remember, you live pretty close to the city. Close enough to check it out and let me know what's going on."

"Do you want me to let you know what's going on, Detective, or do you want me to take care of it?" he asked.

"Let me know," Sara replied. "Because I want to take care of it too."

"Alright," Victor said, scratching the back of his head. "Can I have the address?"

"Sure," she said. "It's off Mansfield Avenue, behind the Crowne Plaza Hotel. Private development. Number 68 Sill Road."

Victor jotted the information down on his pad and said, "Okay. Listen, your number came up as private, and to be honest, I don't have your card anymore."

Sara laughed and told him the number.

"Thanks," Victor said, "I'll put it in my phone when we hang up, and I'll give you a call as soon as I check out her place."

"How are you going to get into the house?" Sara asked.

"Are you asking as a concerned friend or as a detective?" Victor inquired.

"Ah," she said. "Let me know what you find, Victor."

"I will. Bye now."

He ended the call and added Sara's number to his contact list. Standing up, Victor stretched and winced at the way his muscles pulled and complained.

I need to start walking again, he thought and left the room.

"Tom!" Victor called.

The boy didn't answer.

"Tom!" he tried again.

When the teen didn't respond the second time, Victor walked to the boy's room and peeked in. The bed was made, and Tom wasn't there.

Where is he? Victor wondered, turning around and going down into the basement. The boy wasn't working out. *Did he go out with Iris?*

Then Victor shook his head. Iris was away with her family, leaving Tom with little to do over the weekend.

Standing by the young man's pull-up bar, Victor wondered where Tom was.

Victor went back to the study, picked up his phone and checked his text messages. He hadn't missed any from Tom.

Feeling nervous, Victor sent a quick text to the boy.

Where are you?

The reply came through a moment later.

Sorry. I went for a run.

Victor sighed with relief. He had forgotten about the new addition to the boy's workout regimen.

Okay. I have to go out for a bit, Victor wrote. *Are you going to be alright by yourself?*

Yes, Tom responded, and Victor put the phone back on the desk.

Feeling better, Victor searched for Green Tree, Pennsylvania on Google, and clicked the first map that popped up.

Humming, Victor leaned forward and began to read.

***

Tom put his phone away and squashed the feeling of guilt that tried to rise up within him. He hated lying to Victor, but he knew it was a necessary evil.

"Everything good?" Byron asked.

"Everything's good," Tom replied. "Did you bring the stuff?"

The slightly older teen grinned, revealing bad teeth and scarred gums. He gestured to a second teen Tom didn't know, a young man with terrible acne across his forehead.

"Mick," Byron said, "show the man what we brought."

Mick nodded, his dirty blonde hair pulled back in a messy 'man-bun' and removed a large suitcase from the back of a rusted Volkswagen Jetta. Byron's accomplice grunted and struggled beneath the weight of the luggage, the muscles on his neck standing out as he man-handled the case to a position between Byron and Tom. Panting, Mick stepped aside.

"As you can see," Byron said, motioning toward the suitcase, "I did. Did you bring yours?"

Tom nodded and took the cash out of his pocket.

"Damn, son," Byron said, laughing. "That's a serious roll there. Where did you get that kind of money? You stick someone with a jammy?"

"What?" Tom asked, confused.

"A gun, son," Byron said, winking. "Or was it a pretend gun? You know, some paint-gun stripped down to look like a real nine mil.?"

"I didn't rob anyone," Tom said. "A friend gave it to me."

And it was the truth.

Bontoc was a friend, and the dead man had given it to him by telling him where to find the money. The cash had been put aside in case of an emergency while hunting Korzh. His death had precluded him from retrieving it, but not from telling Tom about it.

"Whatever helps you sleep at night," Byron said, chuckling. "Here's the deal. I get a grand for each claymore."

Tom felt the heat of anger spread out from his stomach.

"That wasn't what we agreed on," he said in a low, calm voice.

"That was before I realized how much money you had, yo," Byron said, laughing. "It's a good deal. I mean, Mick and I could always just beat you up and take the money. Then you'd be out of cash and without your little friends."

Tom put the money back in his pocket. His voice remained mellow as he spoke again.

"You're telling me that you and Mick will *take* the money from me?" Tom asked.

Byron's face had gone hard when Tom put the money away.

"This ain't no joke, little boy," Byron snarled. "You best get that cash out and pay me for my merch."

"I just want to be clear," Tom said, and he nodded at Mick. "He's going to help you?"

"Fool," Byron hissed. "Mick—"

Before Byron could finish, Tom moved.

He stepped hard and fast to the right before Mick had time to comprehend what was happening. Within a heartbeat, Tom was in front of the other teen, and he drove his right fist deep into Mick's side.

The result was instantaneous.

Mick's gasp of surprise turned into a scream of pain as he collapsed, hitting the rough dirt road with a thud. Even as he did so, Tom was moving again, reaching Byron in two steps while that teen was struggling to extract a semi-automatic pistol from his waistband.

Tom's fist lashed out and struck Byron's right shoulder.

Byron cursed as his arm went slack, and then he shouted as Tom drove his prosthetic into the other teen's kidney.

Tom watched, perspiration gathering on his upper lip as Byron tumbled to the road, writhing in the dirt on his stomach. Stepping forward, Tom bent down and plucked the pistol out of the waistband. He moved his left arm experimentally and found that the prosthetic was still attached. For several weeks, he had worked on using thin iron bands as an inlay for the false arm. It added weight to the prosthetic, but he knew it would be useful should he encounter any of the dead who weren't particularly friendly.

Tom put the pistol in his own waistband, took hold of the suitcase's handle, and moved away from the two other teens. Once he was a good twenty feet down the road, with both Byron and Mick in front of him where he could see them, Tom opened the suitcase.

Inside were ten claymores mines, each with its trigger. Satisfied, Tom closed the suitcase. It was heavier than he thought it would be, and he knew it would take him longer to get home through the woods.

Straightening up, Tom glanced at Byron and Mick. Byron had gotten into a sitting position, but his arm still hung limply at his side. Mick lay on his good side, weeping and moaning piteously.

"You only have one Goddamned arm," Byron snapped, and Tom could see unspent tears in the young man's eyes.

"All I need," Tom replied. "You should have been fair and kept to the deal."

"Screw you," Byron spat.

Tom shrugged and picked up the suitcase. "Don't come looking for me."

"Or what?" Byron sneered. "You'll kill us?"

"No," Tom said, turning his back on them. "Someone else will."

A chill wind coursed along the dirt road and the two teens behind Tom screamed in horror. The sound made him smile, as did that of Bontoc's voice piercing the peace of the Pennsylvania woods.

CHAPTER 3:
GOING HOME

Stefan Korzh hunkered down in the shadow of a large, fallen oak tree. He adjusted his eye patch giving little thought to it and considered how he might destroy the ghost of his father.

The dead man had promised Stefan the removal of Anne Le Morte and her caretaker.

A single shot, which had missed him only by inches when it smashed through his windshield on his return home, had informed Stefan of his father's duplicity. Part of Stefan admired the way Ivan Denisovich had betrayed him.

It was an act he would have done as well.

His desire to live overruled his admiration, and had he not thrown the truck into reverse and raced back along his driveway, he would be dead.

I'm a fool, Stefan thought, berating himself again.

Focus, he thought, peering out through the undergrowth. *They're both out here.*

Since he returned from delivering the key to his father, and his narrow escape from death, Stefan had spent the majority of his time in the woods hunting for the doll and her human counterpart. He had set several traps, baiting them with fresh meat as he might for an animal. But the woman was wily.

Or else Anne is helping more than I thought she would be, Stefan thought. He took out a small pair of field-glasses and pressed his sole eye to the optics, seeking the slightest hint of the pair.

Nothing, he thought angrily, lowering the glasses a few minutes later.

Using the same amount of care he had employed when traveling to his newest observation post, Stefan retreated. The going was slow, but it was a necessity.

When he reached the outer perimeter of his defenses, Stefan paused. Once again, he considered abandoning the entire complex, but he knew that such an act would only prolong a confrontation, and it would bother him.

He had been afraid of Anne Le Morte. Now he respected her abilities, and he was cautious.

But he wasn't going to run from her.

He wouldn't give her or his father that sort of satisfaction.

I'll jerry-rig a suicide vest and take Anne and her little friend out before I move again, he thought bitterly.

With a sigh, Stefan sank down on his hands and knees, then spread out on his belly, and began the long, worm-like crawl back into the relative safety of the compound.

***

The sun had nearly set when Grace returned to their camp.

"Did you have any luck, my love?" Anne Le Morte asked in French from inside the small tent.

"I saw more meat," Grace replied, sitting down with the old donuts she had taken from the dumpster behind a bakery a few miles away.

"And you left it alone?" Anne asked, as Grace bit into the first of the stale pastries.

"Yes," Grace answered as she chewed. "I was worried I'd get caught. But I want it."

Anne laughed.

"Of course you do," she said, "and you will have more fresh meat soon. I promise."

"Thank you," Grace said, wiping her hands on her pants. "I saw his trail again."

"How far did it go?" Anne asked, her voice intense.

"Within half a mile of our last camp," Grace said. "He'll find it soon enough. I don't know what he'll do after that."

"Hm," Anne said. "Tomorrow, I want you to find another camp. It is deeper in the woods. Farther away."

"You know of it?" Grace asked, unable to silence her surprise.

"Yes, dear one," Anne said, laughing. "I have heard others speak of it. Will you find it for me?"

"I will find anything for you," Grace whispered.

"Mm," Anne said. "Yes. I know you will."

Silence fell over their camp, broken only by the sound of Grace's ravenous eating.

CHAPTER 4

RIGHTFULLY HIS

It hadn't taken long for Gilbert Bray to come to the decision to break into the dead woman's condo.

He was almost positive that his order was there.

The mailman, as far as Gilbert was concerned, was a complete and utter idiot. A fool who happened to be the perfect representative of the postal service, and of federal employees in general.

Gilbert sat in his garage and peered through the half-closed slats of the Venetian blind on the sidedoor's window. He wanted to make certain no one was at the dead woman's house.

Gilbert frowned, upset that he couldn't remember her name. He should, he knew. The police had spoken with her on numerous occasions at Gilbert's behest. She had often played her music too loud, failed to cut her grass or have the rhododendrons in front of her home trimmed in accordance with the policies of the condominium development.

But, in spite of all of these failings, Gilbert still had not wished for the woman's death.

He had often prayed that she would move away, or finally abide by the rules.

Everyone else did, and he couldn't see why she had thought herself above them.

Enough, he thought sourly. *It's time to get what's mine.*

Gilbert leaned over and picked up the pry-bar he had purchased from Home Depot earlier in the day. The side-door into the woman's home had a loose lock, something Gilbert had learned when the Wyborney family had still occupied the residence, and he knew he could get in that way.

With the cold steel in his hand, Gilbert opened his own door and exited the garage. He crossed his own, neatly mown section of lawn onto her wild and unkempt grass, all of which had gone to seed, as had the dandelions and pansies.

God, I hope the next tenants take better care of the yard, he thought, hurrying to her side-door. *Or at least invest in lawn service.*

Concerns over the yard faded away as he stopped at her door, then fit the end of the pry-bar between the lock and the frame and pushed. He heard wood crack and felt the door give way. Slowly at first, then with a loud, hissing crunch, the door sprang open, and Gilbert stumbled into the garage.

Her dark blue Prius was parked and plugged into the charging unit, waiting for a driver who would never return.

The thought turned his stomach, and Gilbert hurried across the silent garage to the interior door. He let out a sigh of relief as the doorknob turned freely and he entered the woman's kitchen. The house felt strange to him, oddly cold, the air heavy.

An uncomfortable sensation filled him, as did a feeling of dread that made him hesitate by the woman's cluttered tabletop.

Fear flickered through him, and he found himself not thinking like a rational 70-year-old, but an irrational child of eight.

She's a ghost, he thought.

As soon as the idea made itself known, Gilbert shook his head and rejected it.

No such thing as ghosts, he told himself, straightening up. *Where's my memorabilia?*

Gilbert focused first on the table and glanced at the two piles of mail. One, he realized, was nothing more than junk. The second consisted of bills.

Was there a third? he asked himself.

There was nothing else on the table and no envelopes on the surprisingly clean counters.

He exited the kitchen and entered the living room, or what had been the living room when the Wyborneys had lived there. Gilbert saw there were two pieces of mail on the coffee table.

Stepping closer to the table, he bent down slightly and saw that the first item was a card. The other was his.

His hands trembled with excitement as he picked up the cardboard shipping envelope. Anger flared for a moment when he realized the woman had opened it, but then he focused on the interior.

The pass for the *Lady Elgin* was there, and in supreme condition, exactly as the seller had described.

Gilbert shuddered with relief, slipped the pass back into the envelope and left the room. Goosebumps erupted on his forearms, and he could hardly contain his excitement. There were so few items concerning the *Lady Elgin*, and he had several of them. Memorabilia from that sinking steamship was far more enticing to him than anything the *Titanic* might offer.

Clutching the envelope to his chest, Gilbert walked towards the side door.

"What are you doing?" a voice asked from behind him, and Gilbert froze, horrified.

Swallowing dryly, he turned around to face the speaker. He planned to apologize, to come up with a lame excuse for having broken into the condominium. Instead, Gilbert's mouth opened, and he let out a shriek reminiscent of a bird of prey, the note high and unyielding.

The terror that sprang into his heart drove him backward.

At the end of the kitchen, in a partially darkened hallway, he saw the woman.

The dead woman.

Her body was pale and wet, her lips no longer red but pale and tinged with blue. The woman's eyes were wide and unblinking, and at that moment Gilbert knew he was wrong.

Ghosts were real.

"Why are you in my house?" the dead woman asked him.

Gilbert couldn't answer, so he turned and fled while the dead woman screamed, "Why are you in my house?!"

By the time he reached his home, Gilbert was weeping and shaking. Fear threatened to rob him of any coherent thinking, He knew he had left the pry-bar in the house, and he didn't care.

The dead woman was still in her home, and Gilbert wouldn't go back in.

Still clutching the boarding pass to his chest, Gilbert sought a safe place to sit and ignore the fact that he had been able to see through the woman's stomach as she stood in the kitchen.

CHAPTER 5

TAKING A LOOK AROUND

Victor glanced over at Tom and asked, "Are you okay?"

"Hm?" Tom blinked and looked at Victor. "Oh. Yeah. I'm fine."

"Okay," Victor said. After a moment, the traffic light turned green, and he stepped on the gas. "So, I'll be back tonight. You'll be good with lunch and dinner?"

"Yes," Tom answered. "Iris will stop by to make sure I eat and all that good stuff."

Victor nodded as they turned onto Iris' street. "Alright then. I'll text you when I get into Green Tree, and when I'm headed back."

"Sure," Tom said, getting out of the car. "Good luck. And be safe."

"I will," Victor said, waving goodbye as the boy closed the door and walked up the long cobblestone path that led to Iris' front door. Victor waited until Tom was let in before he pulled away from the curb and started on his trip.

The traffic from Fox Cat Hollow to Green Tree was light, and within a few hours, Victor found the condominium development that Sara had spoken to him about. He drove around the private roads and found the unit where the odd death had occurred. Victor slowed down and focused his attention on the houses on either side of the condo, and the woods behind it.

I can get to the back of the house through the trees, he realized and felt a pang of guilt. His face burned with shame as he thought about the secret pleasure that breaking into something brought him.

It was an aspect of his personality that he had a difficult time accepting, despite its usefulness.

Satisfied with what he had seen, Victor left the condominium development and searched for a place to park his car that wouldn't draw too much attention.

At least the car's plates are from Pennsylvania, he thought. *That shouldn't make it stand out too much.*

Eventually, Victor parked in the lot of the Crowne Plaza Hotel, took a bottle of water out of his car, and slipped his iron ring onto his finger. He stretched a little to get the kinks out of his back, took a drink, and started the long walk towards the back of the dead woman's house.

After getting lost twice, Victor arrived after 45 minutes of walking.

He remained in the tree line, watching the back of the house, looking for any item that might be out of the ordinary.

Nothing drew his attention, and after half an hour, Victor stood up and approached the home.

He moved toward a back porch and climbed the stairs gently, mindful of where he placed each foot. Some of the boards were soft beneath his feet, the rotting wood threatening to fall apart at his touch. He made it to the top without incident, and Victor was pleased to find the porch in considerably better condition than the stairs.

When he reached the back side, he propped open the screen door and took out the lock pick tools he had made in the basement of his own home. There was a sense of pride and embarrassment as he used them. He had crafted them and they worked the way they were designed to.

Within a minute, he undid the deadbolt, and thirty seconds later, Victor swung the door open.

Immediately, he noticed the chill in the air and felt a strange, electrical sensation ripple along his exposed skin. When he glanced down at his forearms, he saw that the small hairs stood on end, and goosebumps had erupted along their length.

He took a deep breath and let it out slowly before he crossed the threshold.

The woman, according to Sara Milton, had died in the bathtub.

Victor glanced around the room, getting his bearings, and saw the door to the garage was open as if it had been flung wide and forgotten about. He marked it as an item of interest and proceeded further into the house.

Victor found the downstairs bathroom, which lacked a tub, and then he made his way upstairs. Both of the spare rooms had quarter baths, but it was the master bedroom's bath where he found the tub.

His teeth chattered from the cold as he stepped onto the tile. He flicked on the bathroom light and looked around the room, searching for anything out of the ordinary.

"Who are you?" a voice asked from behind him.

Victor turned around and saw a naked young woman standing in the doorway, blocking his exit from the bathroom.

"My name's Victor," he replied, forcing himself to relax. "What's yours?"

She frowned, then smiled. "Nancy."

"Hello Nancy," Victor said. "Do you know where you are?"

"I'm home," she answered. "I shouldn't be."

"No?" he asked.

Nancy shook her head. "I'm dreaming all of this. I should be at my hotel in San Antonio. I think I've got a fever. This is the strangest dream."

"Is it?" Victor struggled to keep his voice neutral.

She nodded. "I wish I wasn't dreaming. I keep feeling cold, and no matter how hard I try, I can't seem to get dressed. Does that bother you?"

He shook his head, and she smiled.

"No, why should it. You're part of my dream," Nancy said. "Goodbye, Victor. I'm going to try and wake up now."

He watched her turn around and leave the doorway, warmth returning to the room.

After a moment's hesitation, Victor hurried out into the hallway, to try and ask her questions about her dreams, to see if perhaps she remembered anything about her death, but Nancy was already gone.

Sighing, Victor went back into the bathroom and sat down on the edge of the tub to gather his thoughts and to try and think of some way he could help the dead woman.

CHAPTER 6

WAITING FOR NEWS

Sara Milton lived alone in a small apartment on the outskirts of Concord, New Hampshire. She was a solitary creature by nature and preferred to work rather than socialize. Her inability to play the political game in small-town politics meant she would never rise above the rank of detective in the police department, and she had made her peace with that.

Sara was more than content to remain a detective, solving crimes and helping to prevent others.

Maybe I'll even teach one day, she thought, smiling. St. Anselm's had an excellent criminal justice program, and she had even been approached by a former coworker who taught at Norwich University in that school's program.

She knew she had a wealth of options when she retired.

The tea kettle whistled, and Sara stood up, twisting first to the left and then to the right, the bones in her lower back cracking loudly. She winced and walked into the kitchen, where she poured the water over the tea and set it aside to steep. As it did so, Sara prepared a small meal for herself, and by the time she had finished putting it in the dining room, the tea was ready as well. She added a fair amount of sugar, topped it off with cream, and soon was seated at the dining table.

Sara read while she ate, rereading *I am Legend* by Richard Matheson, one of her favorite books. It had been the last gift she had received from King Kincaid, and holding it reminded her of the old man and the astounding amount of wisdom he had gained in his lifetime.

She had finished her dinner and her first cup of tea when the phone rang. Surprised, she picked it up and saw that it was Victor Daniels' number on the caller ID.

"Victor," she said when she answered the call. "How are you?"

"A little rattled," he replied, although his voice sounded fine to her.

"What's going on?" she asked, carrying her tea out into the den and sitting down on the couch.

He told her about visiting Nancy's home, and of finding Nancy's ghost.

Sara took a moment to process the information and then said, "Her daughter's still there."

"Yes," Victor stated. "I'm not quite sure what to do. She doesn't even know she's a ghost. To be perfectly honest, Sara, I haven't had to deal with this situation. I don't know what to do next. Is it as simple as telling her to go to the light?"

Sara sighed and said, "I don't know. A friend of mine told me that most of the dead who stayed knew they were dead and didn't care. We never really broached the subject of a ghost who didn't know they weren't still breathing and upright. And you said you didn't find out who or what killed her?"

"No," Victor said. "I have to go back tomorrow and try to make contact with her. I'd like to see what or who killed her."

"Do you think it was intentional?" Sara asked.

"I don't know," he answered. "I wish I did."

Sara took a sip of her tea and said, "Do me a favor and grab a room at the hotel near her condo, okay?"

"I can't do it right away," Victor said.

"How come?" Sara asked, surprised.

"My son," Victor stated. "I've been disappearing a lot lately, and I'm worried about him. Are you coming down?"

"Yes," she answered. "I should be there tomorrow sometime. Whatever flight I can find. I'll text you the details."

"Alright," Victor said. "I'm only a few hours away. I'll drive home, check in on my boy and then come back and meet you at the hotel."

"I can work with that," Sara said. "We'll touch base tomorrow."

She ended the call and put the phone down beside her on the couch. Sara drank her tea slowly and closed her eyes, imagining the steps needed to get down to Green Tree, Pennsylvania.

CHAPTER 7:
IN THE QUESTION ROOM

The room Ariana had designed to serve as a prison for ghosts functioned equally well as a room isolated from them.

On the exterior of the glass, she taped up thick, brown packaging paper, ensuring there was no way to look into the room. With that finished, she brought her laptop in and closed the door. She doubted her father would send anyone to spy on her, but, as Ben Franklin had liked to say, *an ounce of prevention is worth a pound of cure.*

And Ariana did not want any of her father's minions to see what she planned on researching.

Paranoid much? she wondered. But Ariana knew she wasn't being paranoid.

Her father had lived a long time because he had taken precautions. He had been careful.

She hoped to live long as well.

Ariana carried a folding chair into the room, closed the door and set the chair up in front of the computer. She sat down and focused on finding information on ways to destroy a powerful ghost without accidentally blowing up either herself or an acre of land.

Ariana searched for hours, and while she came upon several promising ideas, there was nothing set in stone.

And she wanted a guarantee.

Frustrated, she finally pushed herself away from the computer and rubbed her eyes. The old injuries she had suffered at the hands of Stefan ached, and she felt the urge to punch him.

That's not going to happen, she thought bitterly.

So, Ariana moved on to her next favorite activity.

She picked up the phone and dialed Victor's number.

It rang three times, and he answered it.

"Hello?" his voice relayed how tired he was, but even so, Ariana felt a thrill at the utterance of that simple word.

"Hey there," she said, reclining in the chair.

"Ariana," he said, and his voice tightened. Part of her stomach twisted playfully, and she imagined that the shift in his voice was from some sort of mutual attraction.

"Are you out there hunting my brother?" she asked.

"Not at the moment," he replied.

"Then what are you up to?" she played with a strand of hair and then dropped it when she realized what she was doing, and the biological reason behind it.

"Driving home," he answered. "I need to make sure Tom is doing what he needs to do. School will be starting again soon enough. We both need to start acting like at least part of our lives are normal."

She shook her head and said to him, "Victor, there's nothing normal about your lives. Not since Stefan entered them."

The silence on the other end told her she had gone too far.

She searched for something to say, but Victor's words interrupted her.

"Ariana," he said, his voice strained. "I have to go now. I'm sure we'll talk again."

The call ended, and Ariana was left with the phone in her hand.

Her shoulders slumped, and she closed her eyes.

Stupid, she thought, dropping the phone into her lap. *Absolutely stupid.*

Opening her eyes again, Ariana leaned forward and went back to her search on the web.

CHAPTER 8

A LITTLE IRONING

"How does that feel?" Matthew, Iris' brother, asked.

The young man had driven Tom home, not only because Iris had been called in to work, but to test out the changes made to the prosthetic.

Tom moved his arm experimentally. The additional weight wasn't too noticeable, although he felt certain it would be after a ten-hour day of wearing the prosthetic.

"Good," Tom said, nodding to Matthew.

The two young men sat in Tom's kitchen, and Matthew grinned at Tom's pronouncement.

"Cool." Iris' brother was twenty-one, and he was the only apprentice blacksmith Tom had ever heard of. He had been the one to do the initial inlay of thin iron lines to the arm, and he had agreed to adding one more.

"So," Matthew said, folding his arms over his chest and leaning against the wall, "I think I've earned the right to ask. Why in God's name do you want iron in your prosthetic?"

"Superstition," Tom lied. "Iron is supposed to keep ghosts away. I have this fear of them. It's gotten worse over the past couple of months. From what I read, iron keeps them away."

"Huh." Matthew shrugged. "Okay. If that works for you, then who am I to judge. Anyway, it was fun designing the inlay for the piece. I'm happy with the way it turned out."

Tom lifted his left arm up and looked at the thin lettering that wrapped around the wrist of the prosthetic. The letters spelled out 'SPQR', which stood for *Senatus Populusque Romanus*, the senate and the people of Rome.

It was a cold, bitter reminder of his parents' death at the hands of Stefan Korzh.

And the iron would serve to help defend him against any of the dead who might attack.

"Why Rome?" Matthew asked, interrupting Tom's contemplation.

"Oh, I like ancient Rome," Tom answered. "The legions and all that."

"And your dad doesn't have a problem with it?" Matthew asked. It was a question that he had posed many times since Tom and Iris had first approached him about the task.

"No," Tom said, laughing. "Not at all. He'd rather deal with a decoration on a prosthetic that can be replaced than a tattoo on the only other arm that I have left."

Matthew smiled and nodded. "As long as your dad is cool with it, then I'm happy that you like it. The last thing I want is your dad coming to find me and causing trouble."

"Yeah, that won't happen," Tom assured him. "He's kind of superstitious too."

"Alright," Matthew said. His phone chimed and he pulled it out of his pocket. Matthew read the text and rolled his eyes. "One of the problems of living at home."

Tom raised an eyebrow, and Matthew grinned. "Mom wants a gallon of milk."

"No bread?" Tom asked.

Matthew let out a laugh and shook his head. "No, man. No bread. That was yesterday. Let me know if you want anything else done, this was fun to work on."

"Of course," Tom said. "I'll see you soon."

"You got it," Matthew said, and he left the house.

When Tom heard Matthew's car pull away, he locked the door and moved his arm around several more times.

"It would be best, Tom Daniels," Bontoc said from behind him, "if you kept that arm away from me."

Tom looked at the dead man and nodded. "Yes. I wasn't planning on trying it out on you, Bontoc."

"Were you going to try it out on someone?" Bontoc asked, sitting down on the floor in front of the refrigerator.

"No," Tom replied. "I know what iron can do. I do have a question for you."

"Then ask it," the dead man said, grinning.

"Why did you give me this ring?" Tom lifted his right hand, the fluorescent kitchen light reflecting in the polished aluminum. It was a question he had meant to ask many times before but had never found the courage to question the dead headhunter.

"Ah," Bontoc said, and the humor evaporated from his voice. "That is a deceptively simple answer, my young friend."

"May I know the answer?" Tom asked, sitting down at the table.

Bontoc smiled. "Yes. When I met you, Tom, I saw your potential. You are filled with a singular purpose, and that, as we both know, is to see Stefan Korzh dead and gutted at your feet. I had hoped to do the deed myself. Korzh is, unfortunately, an extremely lucky man. I thought, however, that should I die I would still like to be there at the kill, when the deed is done. And you, my young friend, have the best chance at accomplishing such a task. It does not mean that your luck may be worse than his. In fact, you will need a tremendous amount if you are to succeed. But that is why you have me. Together, we will kill him and satisfy our appetites for revenge."

Tom considered the answer for several minutes, then said, "I don't want to wait any longer."

"Neither do I," Bontoc said. His voice was cold, and for the first time sounded as though it belonged to a dead man.

"Victor's on his way home," Tom continued, "but then he'll be gone again in the morning."

Bontoc nodded. "I think you have enough of a chance now, Tom Daniels. With your arm enhanced with iron, and my ability to speak with Anne Le Morte, I believe we can take Korzh on our own."

"Good," Tom whispered, looking down at his prosthetic and the dull black of the inlaid iron. He shuddered at the memory of Anne Le Morte, but an old proverb came unbidden to him. *The enemy of my enemy is my friend.*

"Good," Tom said again, raising his voice. "It's time he died."

CHAPTER 9

TRAPPED AND CONFUSED

"Go away," Gilbert whispered into the darkness.

He hid beneath his bed, wrapped in a blanket and clad in his winter clothes.

And still, he shivered.

His breath rolled out in great clouds from his lips, and he looked desperately at the closed door to his bedroom.

All he wanted was to reach the door, to escape through it and make his way to the garage.

But he couldn't.

The child wouldn't let him.

A flicker of movement caught his eye and Gilbert squeezed both eyes shut as he screamed, "Go away!"

"You are a mean man," the child said from the bathroom. "I don't like you."

"I don't care!" Gilbert snapped. "Get out of my house!"

"No," the dead boy replied. "No. You remind me of *him*."

When the last word left the child's mouth, Gilbert shuddered.

He didn't know whom the dead boy spoke of, but the hate in the word was enough to know that if Gilbert died, it wouldn't be easy. Not the way it had been for the woman who had drowned.

Murdered, Gilbert thought, pulling himself into a fetal position. *He said he killed her. Drowned her because that's how he died. How everyone died. How I'm going to die!*

Gilbert bit down on his lips to stop himself from screaming.

He felt a tug, and suddenly the blanket was gone, torn from him. Then the bed was lifted and thrown to one side, leaving Gilbert exposed.

His eyes opened of their own accord, and he found himself staring at the grim expression of a barely defined child.

"You're going to die," the child said in a soft, sing-song voice, "and I'm going to help you."

"But I don't want to," Gilbert hissed. "That woman, she deserved it. She stole the ticket from me."

"Don't you know?" the dead boy asked.

"What?" Gilbert asked, his voice shuddering.

"That *deserve* has nothing to do with anything." The dead boy reached down, grabbed hold of the back of Gilbert's shirt and dragged him towards the master bathroom. At the flick of the child's wrist, the door flew open and the drain in the tub snapped shut. Another motion sent the hot water tap spinning and water came rushing forth.

With disturbing ease, the child lifted Gilbert and slammed him down into the tub. Screaming, Gilbert tried to get away, but the dead boy's strength was immense.

Gilbert was thrust under the stream of scalding water pouring from the faucet, the liquid filling his nose and mouth as he gasped for air. The pain was horrific, and for several seconds Gilbert struggled unsuccessfully to free himself.

Suddenly, he was jerked out from beneath the torrent, and as he lay in the tub, the water rising around him, Gilbert sputtered and looked at the dead boy.

"Please," he whimpered.

The ghost smiled and said, "No."

With the water soaking into his clothes and weighing him down, Gilbert could no longer struggle as the boy drove him forward beneath the hot water again.

CHAPTER 10:
DINNER CONVERSATIONS

"This," Victor said, wiping his mouth with his napkin, "is going to sound like the stupidest question of all time."

Tom looked up at him, grinned and said, "There are no stupid questions. Just stupid people."

Victor chuckled and shook his head. "That's a wicked sense of humor, Tom."

The boy shrugged and put another piece of steak in his mouth and as he chewed, Victor continued.

"Are you looking forward to going back to school?" Victor asked.

Tom finished chewing, relaxed in his chair and said, "You know, actually I am. I know it's a few weeks away, and I can remember how much I hated school before everything happened. But now, I think about how nice and normal it will be. Well, as normal as anything can be now."

"Yes," Victor agreed. He looked down at his plate for a moment, pushed a few grains of rice around with his fork and said, "I might even get a job."

Tom laughed and said, "What? You don't want to stay at home and write anymore?"

"No, that's not it," Victor said, smiling sadly. "It's just that I've discovered that too much time alone makes me think of Erin."

Tom nodded, his smile fading away. "I know what you mean."

"I think," Victor said, clearing his throat, "I think that if I get a job, it might distract me a little more."

"What about Korzh?" Tom asked, and Victor heard the hard hatred in the boy's voice.

"A job outside the home will have to wait until that business is taken care of," Victor said softly. "I wouldn't be able to rest if I walked away from that."

They were quiet for several minutes, Victor sipped his water while Tom finished his dinner. When he was done, Victor said, "I have to go away for a few days."

"You know that's not a problem," Tom said. "I can take care of myself."

"I know," Victor replied. "I still worry about you though, Tom."

The boy smiled. "Thanks. I'll be okay though. I mean, I have Bontoc if anything really crazy happens."

Victor offered a tight smile and said, "I hope it doesn't get really crazy then."

"You don't like him." It was a statement, not a question.

"It's not a matter of like or dislike," Victor said after a moment. "It's a matter of trust. I don't trust him. I think he wants something from you, Tom, and I don't think he's going to care what happens to you so long as he gets it."

The boy's face reddened, and he pushed his plate away from him.

"I don't think he will," Tom said, standing up. "He's going to help me find Stefan. And when the time comes, he's going to help me kill him."

Victor watched Tom stalk out of the room, and when the teen was gone, Victor shook his head.

He stared down at his plate and thought, *I wish you were here, Erin. I wish you could help me with this. Hell, I wish you weren't dead. Why was that taken from us? Why were you taken from me?*

He let himself wallow in his depression for a short time, then he stood up and cleared the dishes. He washed and dried them in silence, keenly aware of the absence of sound from Tom's room. Victor had learned that noise meant the boy was alright. When Tom was silent, the boy was crying, and not to be disturbed.

Victor hated the silence.

***

One of many items Stefan Korzh had purchased was a large, full-length mirror.

It hadn't been out of vanity, or a desire to preen in front of it.

The mirror had a simple and practical application.

It allowed Stefan to see if there was any part of his gear that might give him away.

He was clad in all black, the clothes loose and comfortable. Nothing he wore was reflective or could catch the light and reveal him. He had applied face paint the same way. A dull finish in random patterns that erased any semblance of humanity to the passing eye. He had even coated his eye patch with the same paint.

Stefan knew that no amount of camouflage would hide him from Anne Le Morte, but he hoped she would send her guardian out alone.

And that's the only person I need to hide from, he thought, stepping away from the mirror.

Stefan walked to the kitchen counter and picked up his gloves. They were expensive and designed for heavy construction work. He had spent hours removing the protective padding and inserting iron plates into the back of the gloves. The weight was uncomfortable, and they would make firing a weapon nearly impossible.

Which was why he had gathered his knives. He slipped several into different pockets, then he took the last one, a long stiletto and attached it to the chest of his jacket. The handle was facing down so that he could release the safety clip and draw the weapon down all in one motion. An act which could save his life, and had in the past.

No time to think of the past, Stefan thought, leaving the kitchen. *No matter how pleasant the memories might be.*

He focused on his footsteps, pleased when he heard nothing as he walked. The task ahead would be difficult, and he needed every edge he could get over Anne Le Morte and her caretaker.

Satisfied that he had taken every precaution he could think of, Stefan headed for the exit.

Chapter 11:
Obscured

Leanne pushed at the wall, the darkness around her complete. The compartment she had climbed into in her home in New Orleans had been a trap, a power stronger than her seeking to keep her buried in the house. But she had pushed her way forward until she could feel dirt beneath her hands, grains of it embedding themselves beneath her nails. She remembered scrambling ever forward, weakening as humid air made breathing difficult, and she knew she needed to find her way out.

But something more than survival urged her on. Leanne knew that if she were to have her revenge upon Victor Daniels for his part in the death of Jean Luc, then she needed to escape.

Snarling with rage, she clawed at the wall. She felt great chunks of earth scoop out in her hands, each falling to the floor for her to trample and trip upon. Her breathing came in ragged gasps, and her hatred for the world grew with every rasping beat of her heart.

She had been crawling for days, it seemed, and she had lost track of time. A ravenous hunger filled her, and she struggled to escape. Images of vengeance filled her, and then, her hand struck wood.

It was soft and porous beneath her fingers, and with a snarl, she pushed her hand against it. The wood separated with a curious gasp, and the stench of the grave suddenly filled the dark room. Thrusting both hands into the hole, she widened it, the rotten wood crumbling beneath her onslaught. Then, Leanne's fingers closed around old clothes and withered flesh. Clasping the body, she tore a shrunken arm out and dropped it to the floor. She repeated the process again and again, until she had pulled the whole body out of the coffin, and widened the hole so that she could climb up and in.

Once in the rotten interior of the casket, Leanne tore the cover to pieces, dropping each down into the hole to fall upon the corpse whose final rest she had disturbed. Soon, the top of the coffin was missing, leaving only the heavy stone of a sarcophagus above her.

Muttering a foul spell beneath her tongue, Leanne put her hands on the cover and pushed up. For a moment, nothing happened, then the cover shifted, and a hairline crack appeared between it and the base. Panting, Leanne threw the cover aside, enjoying the way it thundered against the floor and smashed into the base of another sarcophagus.

Relief flooded over her, and she sagged against the side of her escape route. Beyond the stained glass of the door's window, she could see the moon high in the night sky.

That's not right, she thought, forcing herself to get out of the grave. She sank to her knees, rested for a moment on the cold marble floor of the mausoleum, then pushed herself back to her feet. Leanne limped to the door and peered out the window.

I should be outside of my house! Fury built within her.

But beyond the stained glass of the crypt, she did not see one of New Orleans' graveyards.

By sight and smell, Leanne understood she was in New England. Far from where she wanted to be. Rage boiled in the depths of her heart, slowly and steadily with all the silence and danger of a fire burning within a wall.

Somehow, she had been cast out of Louisiana.

Finally, Leanne screamed, and the windows in the mausoleum exploded out into the night. She knocked out the last few shards of glass that clung to the framework of the stained-glass window and climbed out into the night. A chill rode along the wind and bit into her ancient flesh, and for a long time, she stood in the cemetery.

Somehow, she had been banished from her homeland, and she doubted she could ever find a way back in.

No matter, she thought, limping toward the narrow ribbon of asphalt road that cut through the cemetery, *I will find Victor Daniels. I will have my revenge.*

Hatred propelled her forward, and she knew it would keep her focused upon her vengeance.

CHAPTER 12:
RIPPLES IN A POND

Polly Rodgers sat on the floor of her bedroom, playing Hero Academy 2 and trying to beat her high score. Allan Gorsch kept sending her text messages and trying to speak with her, but Polly had decided she was through with him.

She muttered a curse under her breath, careful not to let her parents hear it, and slammed the phone down as the Hero app crashed.

"Polly!" her father called up.

She rolled her eyes but made sure her voice was sweet as she asked, "Yeah?"

"Don't slam your phone down!" he answered.

"Okay!" Polly stuck her tongue out at the door and rolled over onto her back.

I'm 13, and they still act like they can tell me what to do, she thought angrily. She stared at the glow in the dark stars stuck to the ceiling and wondered why she had ever thought it was cool to put them up.

For several minutes she lay on the floor, wondering what to do when she heard her mother's footsteps stop outside of her door. Her mother knocked softly and opened the door when Polly sighed, "Hello."

"Hey Polly," her mom said, hesitating, "your father and I are going out. Do you want anything?"

"Could I have a chocolate bar and some Pepsi?" Polly asked, her hopes rising.

Her mother shook her head once and looked away. "You know you can't. The doctor put you on a really strict diet because you're too big. I can't keep getting you junk food."

Polly fought the tears that rose up and said, "Fine."

Her mother paused, then whispered, "Goodbye."

When the door clicked shut, Polly wiped the unspent tears from her eyes, furious with the doctor for putting her on a diet and with her parents for listening to him.

There's nothing wrong with my weight! Polly thought angrily.

She heard and felt the front door close, then a moment later she heard her father's Harley Davidson start up. Seconds after that, the sound of the motorcycle faded as her parents left her alone in the house.

Polly considered a quick trip to the kitchen, to see what might be lying around. But she had tried that the day before.

Her parents had gotten rid of everything she wasn't supposed to eat. There wasn't even any beer in the house for her father. They were all eating the meal plan prescribed to Polly by Dr. Lourde.

Her phone buzzed, and she picked it up.

Y wont u answer????????? Allan's newest text read.

Polly began a reply, and her phone went dead.

She stared at the phone for a moment, then shook it.

The screen remained black.

She pried a thumbnail between the upper and lower casing, popped the back off and took the battery out. Polly blew on it, then slipped the battery back in and closed the case. She pressed the power button, but the phone wouldn't power-up.

Oh. My. God! Polly thought, squeezing the phone in her hand and trying to will it to turn on. She didn't want to talk to Allan, but she did want her phone to work.

Frustrated, she tried to get the phone to power-up, but nothing worked. Finally, with a snort of disgust, she threw the phone across the room and watched with satisfaction as it left a mark in the wall by her door.

Stupid. Everyone and everything is stupid. She got up, walked to her bed and flopped down on it, the mattress and box spring complaining. Goosebumps rose up on her arms, and she shivered. *And they turned the AC up before they left. Great.*

She shook her head and pulled a blanket up over her before she picked up the television remote from her bedside table. Thumbing the power switch, Polly tried to think of what she could watch.

But the television didn't turn on.

She tried it again.

Still nothing.

This is ridiculous, she thought. She dropped the remote to the floor and snatched up her laptop from the table.

The computer wouldn't power-up either.

An uncomfortable feeling settled over her, and Polly put the laptop down on the bed beside her. Her room had become colder, and the door to her bathroom was open wider than she had left it earlier.

And the nightlight, which was on all the time, was dead.

Polly got out of bed and crept to her bedroom door. She reached out, took hold of the doorknob and then snatched her hand back with a yell of pained surprise.

The doorknob had been bitterly cold.

She rubbed her hands together vigorously, then she reached out again. But as her fingers neared the metal, she felt the cold emanating from it and Polly quickly pulled them away.

Weird, she thought, taking a nervous step back. Shaking her head, she turned to go into the bathroom when she saw a shape flicker past.

She froze and every horror movie she had ever seen, every 'R' rated film her parents had expressly *forbidden* her to see, rushed back into her memory.

"Hello?" she whispered, glancing around the room, trying to see where the shape was. "Is someone there?"

A cold finger touched the back of her neck, and Polly screamed, the sound loud enough to hurt her own ears.

She whipped around but found nothing. Her heart beat against her chest, and she whimpered, moving back towards the open door of her closet.

When she was less than a foot away, the closet door slammed shut, and she shrieked.

Without thinking, Polly ran for the bathroom. Once inside, she launched herself against the door, the entire frame shaking as she closed and locked it. She stumbled back, sank down onto the toilet seat, and stared at the back of the door.

I must be sick, she told herself. *This is just a fever. That's it. Mom always says that I hallucinate when I have a fever. It must be that, and stupid Allan is going to be texting me again.*

Her rapid breathing dominated the stillness of the bathroom as the seconds passed. When she thought she was calm, the toilet flushed by itself.

She screamed again and felt instantly foolish.

Polly had hit the lever with her elbow.

She let out a shaky laugh at her own foolishness and got to her feet.

But then the water in the pedestal sink turned on.

Turning, she looked at it, her eyes widening in horror as water filled the basin.

A moment later she saw a face over her shoulder, grinning at her.

Then, before she could react, she felt a hand wrap itself in her hair, and she was slammed face first into the sink.

As she struggled to free herself from the unknown assailant, the water continued to rise.

CHAPTER 13

AN ENTRANCE

They stood outside of the condo that Victor had broken into, but Detective Sara Milton had the keys, which he appreciated.

"What if we don't see her?" Sara asked.

"Then I'd be happy," Victor replied. "I think that it might mean she's moved on."

Sara nodded. "Let's hope for that."

Victor followed her as she led the way up to the front door of the unit, managed to get the key into the lock, and then opened the door.

Like the previous day, cold air rolled out of the home.

"Good Lord," Sara muttered. "It's like a damned freezer in here."

"Yes," Victor agreed. "Not exactly a good sign."

"No," Sara said. "It definitely isn't."

They closed and locked the front door, and Sara tried the lights. She flicked the switches up and down several times, but to no avail.

She glanced at Victor, and he shook his head.

"The stronger the ghost, the more of a drain there will be on the electrical system of a place," he said. "The bulbs could have been blown out when she was killed."

Sara frowned, but nodded. "You said you saw her upstairs?"

"Yes," Victor said.

"Okay." The detective took the lead, and Victor was satisfied to walk behind her.

The house didn't feel the same as it had the day before. There was a deeper chill to the cold.

The interior was dim as they climbed the stairs and Victor realized they should have opened the blinds. What little light they had was thin and weak, and it made him far more uncomfortable than it should have.

When they reached the second floor, Victor extended his hand to point out the way to the master bedroom and stopped.

The dead woman was ahead of them, and she wasn't alone.

An older man stood beside her, and he was dead as well. His thin, moribund face wore an expression of mingled horror and surprise. His clothes, despite their lack of solidity, appeared to be soaked.

"Nancy," Sara said softly, taking a cautious step forward.

Victor squeezed his hand into a fist, making certain his iron ring was still on his forefinger.

The dead woman turned her head slightly to face Sara.

"Is that my name?" Nancy asked.

Sara nodded.

The dead woman smiled. "It seems like a nice name. Was I nice?"

"You were a sweetheart," Sara whispered.

Nancy's smile faltered, her shoulders slumped, and she said, "I know I'm dead."

"Isn't there any way for you to leave? To move on?" Victor asked.

"He won't let me," Nancy answered, looking down at the floor.

Victor's eyes flicked over to the old man beside her.

"Not me, fools," the dead man hissed.

"No," Nancy confirmed. "Not him. The boy. The boy won't let either of us leave. He won't let us see the way out."

"And there are more coming," the old man added. "Many more. He has an entire manifest to fill, and we're but the first to board the *Lady Elgin*."

Sara started to speak, but both ghosts faded, leaving only the living in the hallway.

She turned and faced Victor.

"Do you have any idea what they're talking about?" she asked.

Victor shook his head. "The *Lady Elgin* sounds familiar, but I don't know why. I'll have to look it up when we get back to the hotel."

"I don't want to go back yet," Sara said.

"I wouldn't advise hanging around," Victor said, heading back toward the stairs.

"Why?" Sara asked, following him.

"I am assuming that the two of them told the truth. The boy, whoever he is, will be gathering more of the dead with him. I would rather not be part of the manifest," Victor said.

"You've got a point there," Sara said.

They reached the first floor and left by way of the front door. When they got into the front yard, Victor paused and enjoyed the warmth of the sun on his face. A crawling sensation traveled up his spine, and he turned to look at the condo again.

In one of the top floor's windows, he thought he saw movement and ignored it as best as possible.

It wasn't time to try and free them.

Not yet.

CHAPTER 14

TRAVELING TOWARD THE ENEMY

Tom and Bontoc had been on the road for hours. The car had been kept at the speed limit, and Tom had obeyed every rule of driving. He didn't have his license, and he feared being pulled over and arrested. Bontoc found Tom's concern amusing.

"My young friend," Bontoc said, "you have faced Stefan Korzh. You have survived Anne Le Morte, and here you worry about the police giving you a traffic ticket."

"Listen, I've had 10 claymore mines, plus an unregistered and likely stolen 9mm, hidden in my room," Tom snapped, gripping the steering wheel and checking his mirrors compulsively. "Now, those same and extremely illegal items are in the back. I don't want to go to jail after going through the trouble of getting them and hiding them."

"I would be worried for you if you did," Bontoc replied, chuckling.

"I don't think it's funny," Tom said as Bontoc faded out for a moment as a car passed them on the left.

"I do," the dead man's disembodied voice replied.

"God," Tom muttered. "Why?"

"Because I would not allow someone as insignificant as a police officer to stop us on our task," Bontoc said, and the deadly seriousness in the headhunter's voice reminded Tom of how dangerous the dead man continued to be.

Tom cleared his throat and said, "Yeah. I forgot about that."

"Fortunately," Bontoc said, "I did not."

They were silent for several more minutes, the woods of Pennsylvania forming a beautiful mosaic of varying shades of green on either side of the road.

Tom's phone rang, and he said, "Answer."

A loud beep followed, and Shane's voice filled the interior of the car.

"Tom!" the older man said cheerfully. "How are you, kid?"

"Surviving," Tom answered.

Shane chuckled. "I hear that. What are you up to?"

"Headed out," Tom began, but his phone squawked once and died.

The car sputtered, the electronics flickered, and the engine died. Tom guided the vehicle to the side of the road, keeping it half on the shoulder, with the passenger side tires in the dirt.

"What the hell?" Tom asked, staring at the dashboard as if the car could tell him what happened.

"Ah, I was afraid of that," Bontoc said in an apologetic tone. "I tried not to drain the car and the phone entirely, but it seems that I misjudged my own need for energy. I am sorry, Tom Daniels."

Tom blinked, shook his head, and said, "Are you serious?"

"I am afraid so," the dead man said. "However, if it is any consolation, my young friend, we are exactly where we need to be."

"What?" Tom asked, looking around at the landscape. "How do you know that? We're not even near any exits."

"Because I know," Bontoc answered. "Through those woods on our right. Half a mile in, we will find a dirt road. Follow that for two miles, and we will be on the outskirts of Stefan's lair. From that point on, Tom Daniels, we will need to proceed with extreme caution. Not only will we have to worry about Korzh, but Anne Le Morte and her caretaker as well. Do you understand?"

The rock of fear in Tom's gut told him that he understood, and he nodded to Bontoc.

"Yes," Tom said, looking at the trees along the edge of the road, "I understand."

"Good," the dead man said. "Let us hunt Stefan Korzh."

Tom nodded and opened the driver's side door.

CHAPTER 15:
IN NEW HAMPSHIRE

Aimee Simon ignored the pain in her lower back, the throbbing agony in her knees, and tottered into her garden. Over the low hedges that served as a barrier between her backyard and Edgewood Cemetery, she saw the wrought iron fence and the headstones. The afternoon sun glowed in the polished marble and granite of the various markers and monuments.

Each time she looked at them, Aimee smiled. The small world of Edgewood Cemetery was peaceful, and it was a shame her husband David was buried there.

He had been a brute of a man, and the fact that he had died of a massive heart attack while beating her had been poetic justice. She would have preferred to put him in a pauper's grave, unknown and unloved, but he had paid for his plot and headstone in advance.

Aimee, thus, had not been able to abandon his corpse.

There had been no wake, however. Nor had she held a funeral for him.

Into the ground as quick as you like, she thought, making her way to the large rose bushes, the pink old-fashioned blooms bright and beautiful. *Just like trash, because that's what you are. Trash.*

She paused at the nearest bush, leaned forward and inhaled the heady scent of the blossom. A smile spread across her face, and she closed her eyes, enjoying the feel of the sun on her skin and the scent of the flowers.

This doesn't make up for the abuse, she thought, opening her eyes and turning to continue on towards her garden shed, *but it helps to ease the pain a bit.*

As always, Aimee did her best to push thoughts of David out of her mind, and she had thrust him into a dark corner by the time she opened the shed door. Humming, she rummaged around in the gloom, found her pruning shears and the padded blue kneeler she used. From beneath it, she retrieved her leather gardening gloves, and it took her several minutes to pull them over her arthritic hands.

The pain of the effort made her grimace and hiss, but once they were on, her hands relaxed in the firm support of the leather. Feeling mollified, Aimee left the shed carrying her equipment and went to the closest rose bush. She dropped the kneeler and the shears to the ground and slowly lowered herself as well.

Once there, Aimee waited for nearly a minute for the sharp, agonizing pain to pass, and when it did, she took up her shears. Soon, all of her concerns slipped away, hidden by the joy she found in gardening.

"Your garden is quite beautiful," a soft voice said from behind her.

Aimee knew several important items about the speaker instantly. First, the speaker was a woman. Second, she was from the South. And third, the words were full of a dangerous malice.

Feigning calm, Aimee pushed herself to her feet and faced the unknown intruder.

She managed to suppress her shock at the sight of the diminutive woman in front of her. The stranger was smaller than Aimee, and she wore clothes stained with dirt and grass. Aimee was surprised to see that the woman was older than she was, at least in her eighties. For a moment, Aimee's heart fluttered with compassion, but then she saw the strength and the hatred in the woman's curiously green eyes.

Aimee forced a smile and said, "Thank you. How did you get in?"

"The gate was open," the stranger replied.

Aimee knew it was a lie. The gate hadn't opened since David had died years earlier. Yet even with that knowledge, her eyes flickered toward it, and a gasp escaped her pursed lips.

The gate was wide open, the lock hanging from stripped screws.

"How did you open the gate?" Aimee asked, confused.

"I didn't," the stranger replied. "It opened for me, as most doors do."

Aimee shook her head. "It couldn't have. I... I think you need to leave."

"No," the woman said, smiling softly. "We've only just met. Ah, but where are my manners. I am Leanne Le Monde. And what's your name?"

"Aimee Simon," she replied, unable to stop herself from answering. Aimee felt as though Leanne had reached in and plucked the name from her mouth.

"See, Ms. Simon," Leanne said, almost purring. "We are like old friends, are we not? Tell me, what will you do with that car in your garage?"

"I want you to leave," Aimee gasped, struggling with the words. Her hands clenched convulsively. "Get out of my yard."

A snarl curled the lips of Leanne, and she spat, "I'll leave when I'm ready, and I will not be ready until you give me the keys to your car. And money. I'll not be able to find Daniels without either of those."

Aimee shook her head. "No. Get out!"

Leanne stepped forward, a quick light step, the sight of which caused Aimee's brain to scream, *Danger!*

Aimee tried to step back but found she couldn't.

She was frozen in place, only her eyes darted around, seeking someone in another yard.

Anyone.

Then Leanne Le Monde was there, her breath hot on Aimee's cheek as the older woman hissed, "Oh, I hate you all. Each and every one of you, from the oldest man to the youngest child. I hate you all."

Aimee couldn't reply, nor could she stop Leanne as the older woman's hands wrapped around Aimee's throat, drew her in close, and bit down upon the woman's ear.

Leanne was pleased with how easily it tore away.

CHAPTER 16:
A PLAN OF HER OWN

Ariana dried off her hair, combed out the knots and she walked into her kitchen. She reached for the vodka, hesitated, then decided on a glass of water instead.

Clearheaded for this next part, she thought. *That's what I need to be.*

She adjusted the tie on her robe, poured her water, and went back to her laptop in her bedroom. Ariana eased down into her chair and stared at the side-by-side windows she had left up on the screen.

Multiple missing person reports. All of them centralized in one area of western Pennsylvania. The police had found absolutely nothing, but the internet was, at times, nothing more than a giant office with people exchanging rumors in the breakroom.

Ariana had sifted through the rumors and found something.

A young woman and her fiancé had gone missing after going out for a hike.

Three hunters vanished over a period of weeks.

Some residents stated that partially eaten remains had been found, and that the police were withholding information.

The police, of course, denied any such discoveries.

Ariana had even found a link on a hacker's website that let her tap into a local gas station's security feed, and she had seen a filthy, unkempt woman rummaging through the garbage.

Anne Le Morte had been in the woman's arms.

But the acreage, Ariana thought, frowning as she magnified the map of the area where the disappearances had occurred. *Easily three hundred. Maybe even more. I'd need a cadaver dog. And a tracker.*

Groaning, she sat back in the chair, running fingers through her damp hair. She glanced at her cellphone, considering a call to Victor, but shoved the thought away. Instead, Ariana leaned down, opened her purse, and removed the compact her father had given her.

She pressed the latch, and when the upper portion sprang open, Ariana brought the mirror up to her mouth and whispered, "Father, remember the watch."

In the space of a heartbeat, a chill descended on the room, and the lights flickered. She quickly stabbed the power button on the laptop and set it into sleep mode lest she lose her work. A second later, Ivan Denisovich Korzh was a dark shadow in the room.

"Ah, my dear child," her dead father said, chuckling, "what is wrong?"

"I think I may have found Anne Le Morte, and in turn, I think I found Stefan," she said, shivering in the sudden cold.

She could hear the smile in his voice as he said, "Excellent! Where is he?"

"Still in Pennsylvania," Ariana answered, "but it's a big area. I was wondering if you knew how I could get in touch with Anne."

"You cannot," he answered, "but perhaps I can. I will try later when we are finished. Tell me, though, how is your friendship with Victor Daniels?"

"It isn't going well at all," Ariana replied, somewhat stiffly. "If anything, I'd say I'm lucky if we still have a work relationship."

"Ah," her father said. "That is a pity. Some things, they cannot be helped. So, I will seek out Anne Le Morte and speak with her about you, and about where you might find my son. Be ready, daughter, my call may come at any time."

Ariana gave him a tight smile.

"Father," she said, "I've been ready for years."

His laughter lingered in the room as the lights brightened and warmth returned.

And once again, Ariana was alone.

CHAPTER 17

AN UNTENABLE LEVEL OF FRUSTRATION

Victor stood on the small porch attached to his hotel room and looked out at the trees that separated the hotel from the condo development where Nancy had been murdered.

Who are you? he thought, trying to imagine the unknown ghost. *Why complete a manifest?*

A hot wind curled in around him and sweat sprang into existence on the back of his neck. With a grumble, he turned around and returned to the cool depths of his room. He closed the sliding door, locked it, and drew the heavy curtain, instantly plunging the room into a pleasant gloom. From his bed, he picked up his cellphone and checked to see if he had any messages from Tom.

There weren't any, and Victor wasn't certain if that was good or bad. Tom was an independent young man, far more adept at navigating life's more mundane problems than most teens his age.

But that makes it all the more worrisome, Victor thought, stretching out on his bed and placing the phone beside him.

Tom's baseline for what he considered dangerous was higher than most adults.

I have to trust him, Victor sighed. *I really do.*

He tried to focus on the situation at hand and recalled the unrewarding conversation he had shared with James Moran. No one on staff at that establishment had even heard of a ghost from the shipwreck of the *Lady Elgin*, let alone of any drowned ghost in search of filling a ship's passenger manifest. James would keep an eye out, of course, and ask around the darker corners of the collecting world, but Victor didn't hold much hope that such inquiries would bear fruit.

Which leads me to my main concern, he thought grimly. *What will happen to those ghosts who were created by the child? How many more had been made?*

Victor had searched for several hours on the internet, but it had been an ultimately fruitless exercise. Then, as a last resort, he had focused on the shipwreck itself, and that information had been less than pleasant.

A hard knock on the hotel room's door interrupted his thoughts and forced Victor to sit up.

"Victor," Sara said from the hall. "Are you in there?"

"Yes," he said, getting off the bed. "Hold on."

He went to the door and let the detective in, the woman giving him a nod and a tired grin. In her hand, she held a tray with a pair of coffees.

"Thirsty?" she asked.

"Definitely," he replied, closing and locking the door behind her. She handed him a cup and held onto one for herself. Sara sat down in one of the room's two chairs and waited for Victor to join her.

"You take cream and sugar, right?" Sara asked, freeing her own cup from the tray and popping off the thin lid.

"I do," Victor replied, sitting down across from her.

"Good," she said. "Mine's black."

"Thank you," Victor said, removing the lid from his own cup.

"You're welcome," Sara replied. "So, I was talking with the local police. Seems like someone used a pry bar and broke into Nancy's house the day before we looked in there."

"Oh?" Victor kept his voice and his face neutral. "A pry bar seems a little excessive for a simple deadbolt."

She shook her head. "I didn't think you had it in you. You don't look the type. Or act like it."

Victor nodded, and Sara dropped the subject of illegal entry.

"As much as I appreciate the coffee," Victor said after a pause, "what brings you by?"

"I was at the police station," Sara said, "expressed my interest in the case since I was a family friend. As I was speaking with the lead investigator, I overheard a conversation about a man named Gilbert, who managed to drown, fully dressed, in his own tub."

"The man we saw with Nancy?" Victor asked.

"I assume so," Sara replied. "And they were also discussing the drowning of a teenage girl in her own bathroom. Not in the bathtub. I don't know how exactly, but it seems to be the same MO. Severe frostbite to strange parts of the body and drowning."

"That is some decidedly unpleasant and depressing news," Victor said with a sigh.

Sara nodded. "So, what information did you pull up on the ship?"

"That's even worse," Victor said. She raised an eyebrow, and he continued.

"The *Lady Elgin* sank on September 8, 1860," he said. "She was a paddle steamer on Lake Michigan, and she was rammed by a schooner during a storm. They think upwards of 300 people died."

Sara blinked several times, shook her head, and asked, "They think?"

"Yes," Victor said. "The passenger manifest was lost when she went down. They have no idea how many people were aboard."

"Evidently this boy knows," Sara murmured. "Would it help if we knew who he was?"

"I don't think so," Victor answered. "I have two main concerns right now. One, finding out what he's attached to and getting a hold of it. Two, what to do about the ghosts he's bound to himself."

"They won't just be freed if we destroy whatever it is?" she asked.

Victor shrugged. "It really could be as simple as that. Or, we might be condemning them to an eternity of wandering. Or we might destroy them as well. I don't know."

Sara groaned. "Damn. Alright. Do you know of anyone who we could talk to about this?"

"No," Victor said, then he straightened up. "Scratch that. Actually, I might."

"Betty Crocker?" Sara asked with a raised eyebrow.

"Possibly," Victor said, "but not who I was thinking of. She's a bit of a wildcard."

"You don't say," she said dryly.

Victor gave her a grin and said, "Yes, I know that's an understatement. No, this is someone else. I'll reach out to him."

"When?" Sara asked.

Victor glanced at the clock on the bedside table and said, "About an hour or two. I want to make sure he's home, and relaxed."

"Okay," she said, nodding. "Want to grab something to eat?"

Victor thought about it for a moment.

"Yes," he said. "Let me get my stuff."

He set the coffee down and stood up. A gut feeling told him that dinner with the detective would have none of the awkwardness of dining with Ariana, and he smiled.

Life, he thought, *might not get any worse.*

CHAPTER 18

ROOM 322

At 49 years of age, Nuala Deanne felt each and every hour she had lived.

Especially after a conference for physical trainers.

Who picked this part of Pennsylvania? she wondered, dropping her bag onto her bed and collapsing beside it. Her feet ached, and her lower back was sore. *Too bad they don't have a masseuse here.*

For several minutes, she remained prone on the bed, then, with a groan of discomfort and general malaise, Nuala rolled over onto her back and sat up. Bending down, she untied her sneakers, kicked them off, and wondered if she even had the energy to make it from the bed to the over-sized hotel bathtub.

Yes, she thought, getting to her feet and wincing at the pain. *You can always make it into a bath.*

Nuala stripped off her clothes as she went into the bathroom, and made a distinct point of not looking at herself in the mirror. Seeing her reflection reminded her that she was a good twenty pounds overweight and that she needed to change her eating habits.

Never good for a trainer to look like she can't take care of herself. Nuala started the water for the tub, used the thermostat to raise the temperature in the bathroom to a comfortable 78 degrees, and climbed into the bath. She shivered for a moment as she adjusted the water's temperature, and then she felt the pain in her feet begin to subside as warm water spilled over them. Nuala curled and uncurled her toes, and then settled back and listened to the tub fill.

One more day of 'how to get the best performance out of your client', she thought. *Then I can drive home and be back to work. And hopefully, there won't be any more bull from Kenneth's lawyer waiting for me.*

Nuala frowned at the thought of her soon-to-be ex-husband, but she didn't bother to chase the thought away. She knew that she would expend more energy trying not to think of him, and then end up thinking about the situation anyway.

For 25 years, they had been married, and then, on their silver anniversary, he had presented her with divorce papers and the information that he was leaving her for his 19-year-old secretary.

He's a walking cliché, Nuala thought bitterly. She blamed herself, of course, and she fought hard to remember that his failings as a person weren't a reflection on her. He would tell everyone who listened that she was a nag, but the reason behind the divorce was more than his lust for a teenager.

For the past six years, Nuala had earned more money than Kenneth, and significantly more with each year. He had a corner office, with his own secretary, but that was because he rented a corner office, and he worked as a mediocre insurance salesman. The BMW he drove had been bought with Nuala's money, not his.

Ugh, Nuala thought, *that's enough. I can think about him later. Right now, I just need to relax.*

No sooner had the thought finished than the lights flickered and went out. The heat died as well.

The water continued to rush out of the faucet, and Nuala closed her eyes. *You've got to be kidding me. I just want a bath. They better not be evacuating the building.*

When almost a minute had passed without the light or heat coming back on, Nuala sat up in the tub. She shivered at the chill in the room and slid back down until the water was almost at her chin.

I wonder what's going on? she thought. She didn't hear anything from the hallway, and neither her cell phone nor the hotel room's phone rang. There was no fire alarm, and nothing seemed out of the ordinary other than the sudden failure of the light and heater.

Nuala leaned forward, turned off the faucet, and quickly sank back into the water. Steam rose up from the water's surface, and she realized the room was far colder than when she had first entered it.

Maybe I should see what's going on, she thought, and when she turned to look for the towels, Nuala froze.

A small figure stood in the bathroom doorway.

The outline was that of a child, but for some reason, Nuala couldn't explain, there was no real definition to it.

The steam, she thought. Then a rational part of her demanded, *why is there a kid in my room?*

"Hey there," Nuala said. "How did you get in?"

The child stepped into the bathroom, and the temperature plummeted. As it drew nearer, Nuala could make out the face of a young boy whose fine, high cheekbones highlighted the depth of his hazel eyes. His hair was long, almost to the collar of his plain white shirt, and he tilted his head slightly to the right as he looked at her.

"Who are you?" the strange child asked. His voice was hollow, sounding as if it came from a great distance rather than a few feet away.

"My name's Nuala," she answered, wondering if there was something wrong with the boy. "Are you okay? Are you lost?"

"I don't know," he said.

"Listen, just look away for a moment, and I'll get a towel on," she said. "Then we can find your mom or dad, whoever you're here with, okay?"

The boy smiled. A soft, beautiful smile that caused Nuala's heart to ache.

"You look like my mother," he said. "She tried to save me."

As Nuala watched, the boy vanished, as if wiped from the face of the world.

CHAPTER 19

FRONT TOWARDS ENEMY

The pack's straps cut into Tom's shoulders, and sweat caused his shirt to cling to his back. He stopped, freed a bottle of water from a side-pocket and took a quick drink. As he put the bottle back, he asked, "How much farther?"

"Not much," Bontoc replied. The dead man was a slim shadow between a pair of trees, more a hint than anything else. "I'm going to go ahead again, to see if I can find where Anne and her caretaker are. I do not wish for us to run into them. Continue along this game trail, my young friend. I will meet up with you soon."

Tom grunted in reply and shook his head as Bontoc slipped away.

He's so strange today, Tom thought, then he chuckled. *When isn't he strange?*

Still smiling, Tom focused on the trail and followed it deeper into the woods.

***

"Where is your mistress?"

The sharp-voiced question caused Grace to jerk upright, her hand on the shotgun and her heart pounding.

"I am here," Anne Le Morte said in French from the confines of the small tent. "What brings you back to us, Bontoc?"

Grace watched as a tall, mangled ghost stepped out of the trees to stand before her. He gave her a grim smile that turned even her hardened stomach, and she looked away. The dead man laughed and answered in French.

"I will ask of you a favor," Bontoc said. "I have a young friend who comes to slay Stefan Korzh."

"He cannot," Anne said snapped.

"I did not say he would be successful," the dead man purred. "I merely stated his purpose."

"Good," Anne replied stiffly. "I had thought, for a moment, that death had caused you to forget mine."

"Not at all," Bontoc said good-naturedly. Then the humor vanished from his voice as he stated, "I merely come to state that you remember our bargain. I am to be at least a witness to his death."

Grace smiled as Anne let out a beautiful, crystalline laugh. "Of course, I have not forgotten. It is a pleasant piece we have negotiated. Your young friend, is he part of the larger plan?"

"He is now," Bontoc stated. "Once the relationship was discovered it was decided that he would be an effective tool to leverage one against the other."

"So, I have been informed as well," Anne said. "Yes, Grace and I will leave your young friend alone. And you, what shall you do?"

"Watch," Bontoc answered, and the grin that spread across his face chilled Grace to her marrow.

***

Stefan's head jerked up as the sensor went off. His eye darted about the different screens until he found the sector with the intruder.

What the hell is that? he thought, leaning forward. He used the keyboard to increase the magnification on the camera and shook his head, dumbfounded at what he saw.

A teenager stomped along one of the many game trails that cut through the property. As the boy drew nearer to the camera, Stefan saw the butt of a semi-automatic pistol protruding from the teen's waistband. There was a fierce, determined expression on the boy's face, and it took Stefan only a moment to understand that the teenager was coming for him.

How did you find me? The question was followed by a burst of anger, and Stefan knew he needed an answer.

Furious, Stefan got out of his seat and hurried out into the kitchen. With well-practiced movements, he put on his body armor and picked up his most recent acquisition, a police-grade Taser. He holstered a semi-automatic .22 on his belt and left the safety of his quarters. Quick steps brought him to a small door he had built over the previous weeks and opened it cautiously.

For a moment, the thought that the teen on the camera might be part of a larger trap flashed through his mind, then Stefan shook the idea away. From what he had seen of Anne Le Morte's caretaker, working as a team player didn't seem to be her strong point.

Stefan took a deep breath and sprinted across the parking lot. When he drew close enough to the fence, he leaped up and caught hold of it. He scrambled upwards, worked his way over the barbed wire with ease, and dropped down to the other side. Within seconds, he was racing towards the tree line.

The lack of a gunshot after him helped him to relax mentally, but he didn't slow down his pace, not until he was in the safety of the woods. His memory of the property's vast layout sprang to the forefront, and he adjusted his direction to a course that would bring him in behind where the trespasser was.

Stefan slowed to a jog when he found the game trail, and when he reached the camera where he had seen the boy, Stefan slowed to a quick walk. His eye focused on where the teenager should be, and soon he saw the back of the boy's head.

With silent footsteps, Stefan crept up to within six feet of the teen, and when the trespasser paused to get a drink of water from his pack, Stefan dropped to one knee, drew his Taser, and whispered, "Hey there, boy."

CHAPTER 20

DINNER

As they waited for dessert, Victor picked up his phone and called Shane Ryan.

The other end rang once before Shane answered.

"I was about to call you," Shane said.

"Is everything alright?" Victor asked.

"I was going to ask you the same thing," the other man said. "I was on the phone with Tom a little while ago, and we got cut off. I gave him half an hour, and when he didn't call back, I tried his phone. It's going right to voicemail."

An uncomfortable wave of fear washed over Victor. "How long ago?"

"About an hour and a half," Shane said. "Where are you?"

"Connecticut," Victor answered. Panic replaced the fear, and he fought to keep it under control. "He was supposed to stay inside."

"Hell, Victor," Shane grumbled. "He's not with you?"

"No," Victor said, "he's home alone."

"Don't worry then," Shane said, chuckling. "He's a teenage boy. He's probably turned his phone off, so he can have some quality time with that girlfriend of his."

Relief swelled within Victor, and he let out a shaky laugh. "Yes. Yes, that's more than likely what he's done."

"Hell, I would have," Shane said, laughing. "Listen, do you need me to go and check on him?"

Victor hesitated, then replied, "No. No, he would think I didn't trust him. I'll give him a little while longer and if he hasn't responded, I'll take you up on the offer."

"Sounds good to me. So, now that we've solved that little mystery," Shane continued, "what were you calling about?"

Victor let out a shaky laugh and explained the situation with Nancy and the other ghost.

"Damn," Shane said after Victor had finished. "That's a tough one. Let me look into it and get back to you, alright?"

"Sure, that would be great," Victor said. "I'll look forward to it."

Victor ended the call and sent a text to Tom.

Are you alright?

He made sure the volume was up, then he placed the phone on the table.

"Is everything alright?" Sara asked.

"I hope so," Victor answered. "My son, he's not answering his phone."

"I'm sorry," she said. "Do you need to go back to the hotel room and try to call him?"

Victor shook his head. "I sent him a text. There's a better chance he'll respond to that than a call. And speaking of calls, Shane will let me know when he finds out any information about a ghost who is bound to another."

"Okay," Sara said. "Do you think it's worth going back out there tonight?"

"To Nancy's house?" Victor asked.

Sara nodded.

He thought about it for a moment, then realized he was the one who had to make the decision. Before he had always relied upon someone else. Jeremy or Shane, even Ariana.

And now myself, Victor thought.

"Yes," he said. "Let's go back there tonight. Maybe, just maybe, we'll get lucky and one of the ghosts can remember something about what the killer might be bound to. It's a longshot, since they're both, well, freshly dead. But it's better than nothing."

"Okay," Sara said, "that sounds good to me."

She turned in her seat and waved the waitress over for the check.

CHAPTER 21:
BITTER DRAUGHTS

There had been little that Leanne found palatable in the old woman's house, but she ignored the foul, tasteless edibles and fed herself.

The old woman's corpse was in the shed, and twice already Leanne had been forced to chase off a large raccoon. She had been left exhausted each time.

Lying on the old woman's bed, Leanne kept her eyes closed and tried to find the reason why her powers had diminished so. She had attempted to scare the raccoon off with a simple spell, and she had failed utterly. Leanne had been forced to resort to banging a pan against the metal of the screen door, and even that had left her arms aching.

Such attempts will not work tonight, she thought. The raccoon would be in his element, and it would have no fear of her.

She inhaled deeply through her nose, exhaled from her mouth, and fostered a sense of calm. It soon became a reality, and she was able to sink down into the darker parts of herself, the places in her mind where her power had its roots.

And it was gone.

Her eyes snapped open, her heartbeat quick against her breastbone.

Where is it? she thought, and for the first time in her exceptionally long life, Leanne Le Monde was truly afraid.

The image of her power as a tree, with roots, set deep in her heart, had long been a tool for her to use. But when she had searched out that hallowed grove, the tree was gone. The roots stripped from the earth and the churned earth liberally salted so that nothing would grow there again.

Where, she began to ask herself again, and then she stopped herself.

Leanne knew where. She even knew when.

Coming through the coffin and into the inner sanctum of the mausoleum. Only there could it have been stripped from her. A simple and effective trap for one as proud as herself.

She pushed herself up, panting for breath by the time she finished. Sitting on the edge of the bed, her head hung down and her chin against her chest, a dull, horrible realization filled her.

I will have to get to Victor Daniels as an old woman, she thought, clenching her teeth. *I will need to slay him as the same. Jean Luc will be avenged.*

Leanne knew that if her friend had not died, then she would not have had to try and seek justice or assistance from others. And if she had not done that, her power would have remained intact.

Victor Daniels, she knew, had a tremendous amount to answer for.

And he will, Leanne thought, getting to her feet and staggering to the bathroom. *He will.*

From the backyard came the sound of the raccoon scratching at the shed.

CHAPTER 22:
IN THE JUNGLE

His prosthetic was gone.

Tom felt nauseated as he tried to piece together where he was.

But he neither saw nor heard anything.

With his right hand, he reached up and searched his face for a blindfold or a mask, something that would explain why he couldn't see. It took him only a moment to understand that he was in a room, without any sort of light. He was propped up at the junction of two walls, his legs stretched out, and his feet pressed into another corner. Placing his hand on the floor, Tom felt cold wood.

This isn't good, he thought, putting his hand back into his lap.

As he considered his situation, the sound of footsteps stopped near him.

A click sounded, and then from a speaker above him, came a man's voice.

"Hello," the stranger said, "who might you be?"

Tom made a rude gesture in the darkness, and his unknown captor let out a chuckle, letting Tom know that the man had night vision capabilities on a camera focused on his cell.

"Excellent," the stranger said. "I like your spirit. We'll have a longer chat later on."

The audible click of a speaker being turned off filled the room and then left Tom in silence.

He closed his eyes, rested his hand on his lap, and waited to see what would happen next.

***

Stefan stood at the small monitor on the exterior of the cell for a minute longer and looked at the boy shown on the screen in the strange green glow of the night vision lens. The teen, Jeremiah Daniels, according to the information in his wallet, had closed his eyes and seemed prepared to wait.

The urge to go in and strangle the boy was strong and it was with some difficulty that Stefan restrained himself.

A hunter going missing in the woods of Pennsylvania is one thing, Stefan thought. *A missing teen, especially one with only three limbs, will cause a disturbance. I don't need the police and law enforcement crawling around all over the place.*

Stefan had a mental image of the police on all fours, searching for the boy, and chuckled as he walked away from the small cell.

He had constructed it on the off-chance that he might need to question someone again, and after the debacle with his half-sister, he didn't want to be caught unprepared again.

Stefan went into his bedroom, closed and locked the door, and sat down on his bed. He picked up the teen's prosthetic arm and examined it.

The device was finely crafted, an obviously high-end piece of medical equipment. But what interested Stefan the most was the iron that had been attached to the piece. He ran his thumb over the *SPQR* that had been inlaid at the wrist and wondered what the boy had been through.

And what have I done to him to cause him to come looking for me? Stefan wondered. He didn't doubt that he had done something to anger the teen. The boy had the stamp of vengeance on him, and there was a nagging sense that he had seen the boy somewhere as well.

More importantly, Stefan thought, setting the prosthetic back down on the bed. *How did he find me? How did he get past Anne and her caretaker?*

For that matter, how did I?

Stefan shook his head. He didn't like all the unanswered questions.

Other than the boy, the whole situation had the markings of a trap.

And that caused Stefan to worry.

***

Grace stood with Anne and looked at the warehouse where the prey lived.

The dead man, Bontoc, sat on the ground beside her.

"He may discover that his barrier has been breached," Anne said, breaking the silence.

"He may indeed," Bontoc agreed, "but that would be of no significance. Eventually, they will come, and the barrier would be disturbed again. Enough to allow you ingress."

Anne laughed in her sweet way and said, "That is true. And you will not kill him?"

"Not without you," Bontoc affirmed. "We have made a bargain, Anne Le Morte. I will keep my end of it."

"And I mine," Anne said. "Soon our tasks will be complete, and I will be free to roam once more."

Bontoc nodded.

"Tell me," Anne said with a hint of a smile in her voice, "do you not feel remorse for your betrayal?"

"Betrayal?" Bontoc shook his head and laughed. "Tom Daniels is a smart boy. And a strong one. I admire him. I hope he will survive this, for I think it will be entertaining to see what damage he can wreak upon the world. I shall shed no tears, however, should he die. In the end, he is nothing more than a tool. And a tool, dear lady, should hope for nothing more than to serve its purpose."

Grace adjusted Anne in her arms and returned her gaze to the warehouse, wondering when it would be time to go in and kill the one named Stefan Korzh.

CHAPTER 23

EMPTY HOUSES

Barbara Goss walked down the sidewalk and glanced to either side as she did so. The air felt wrong, almost heavy. Above her, the street lights weren't as bright as they normally were, and she passed a house without any lights on.

She stopped and looked around.

The small cul-de-sac was silent. She didn't hear any dogs. There was a distinct lack of voices coming from backyards or decks.

Barbara had never heard the cul-de-sac quiet before, and it had been part of her evening walk for fifteen years.

Cars were parked in the driveways, and six of the eight houses were completely dark.

And as she watched, the seventh house went dark. As if someone had gone into the basement and thrown the master-switch on the breaker box.

What is going on here? she thought.

An uncomfortable, nervous feeling swelled up within her, and she struggled against a sense of fear.

Barbara looked at the last house, which belonged to Bill Ross, a man who had been friends with her ex-husband for many years. As she bit on her lower lip, not sure what to do, the lights in Bill's house flickered.

She continued to stand on the edge of the road, hesitant until she saw Bill's door open a few inches, and then no more.

Something inside of her strengthened and Barbara walked towards the front of Bill's house.

There might be a gas leak, she thought. *Something dangerous.*

Barbara pushed those frightened ideas away and focused on the one that grew steadily within her.

If there's a gas leak, she thought, *then Bill needs help.*

By the time she finished the thought, Barbara had reached Bill's front yard. Without any more hesitation, she hurried up the walkway to the steps, climbed them and knocked on the door frame.

"Bill?" The house went dark as she called his name. She licked her lips nervously, knocked again and said, "Bill, is everything okay in there?"

Barbara pushed the door open a few more inches, stepped closer and called out, "Bill?"

As his name left her mouth, Barbara saw him laid out on the floor of the hallway. He was on his back, arms and legs wide.

And there was a puddle of water around the man, his clothes soaked. A glistening trail led away from him and back to the first-floor bathroom.

Bill! she thought, and rushed into the house. Her fear for him set her entire body to shake with chills, and she sank down to her knees in the puddle beside the man. Frightened, Barbara reached out, found his wrist, and took his pulse.

She dropped his arm with a whimper of revulsion.

His flesh had been wet and bitterly cold, and there hadn't been the faintest hint of a pulse.

It was then she noticed how cold it was in the house, but Barbara didn't hear any air-conditioner running. All the ambient noise was gone, as were the lights.

She got to her feet and made her way to the door. When she crossed the threshold and stood on the front steps, she breathed a sigh of relief.

I need to get home, she thought, fear welling up and threatening to strip her of reason. *I need to call the police. I have to be somewhere safe.*

Barbara turned around and let out a high squeal of dismay.

A young boy stood on the walkway between her and the street.

Between her and home.

"Hello," she said, clearing her throat. "Do you live around here?"

A soft smile graced his fine features, and he shook his head. "I don't live anywhere."

"Are you homeless?" Barbara asked.

"Yes," the boy said after a moment. Then he added, "But I also don't live."

"What?" she asked, confused.

"I'm dead," the boy said. "Like the man in the house you just left. And the family in the house beside his. And the one in the house across from theirs. They're all dead. Like me. I made them that way."

Barbara let out a shaky, nervous laugh.

But then she realized that she shouldn't have.

There was no humor in the boy's voice, or in his face.

She quickly descended the stairs, glancing around, searching for a place to run to. The boy was small, but she didn't doubt he would be able to harm her.

There was a sense of *wrongness* about him.

Barbara edged towards the left, and while the boy didn't move towards her, his eyes never left her face. When she reached the sidewalk, she glanced to the street, then back to the boy, and he was in front of her, within arm's length.

Barbara screamed a short, sharp sound that was silenced in an instant when she clamped a hand over her mouth, trying to stifle her own fear.

A small smile appeared on the boy's face, and he said, "You can scream if you want."

"Why?" she whispered.

"Because," the boy said, stepping closer, "it's going to hurt, and no one will hear you."

Barbara realized the boy was right and she tried to run.

The strange child was on her in a heartbeat, hands grasped the back of her sweater and pulled her down. She tried to scream, but only a strangled cough escaped her lips, the collar of her sweater pressing brutally upon her windpipe. The boy dragged her backward into the house, and she broke her nails as she clawed at the walls, seeking for some way to stop her inevitable progress.

A moment later the child pulled her up the stairs, over the threshold, and past Bill's body. The water was cold against her hands, and she tried to scream again as they entered the bathroom. For a split second, her hands latched onto the doorframe, but the boy merely laughed and yanked her through. Slivers of wood broke away and gouged her fingers.

Suddenly, the boy flipped her over onto her stomach, and before she could stop him, he thrust her face into the toilet, sighing happily as he did so.

CHAPTER 24

DUTY CALLS

"You can't be serious," Sara said into her phone.

They stood in the parking lot beside Sara's rental car.

Victor watched as furrows appeared on the woman's brow.

"Alright," she said, nodding. "Yeah. Yes, I said. I'll be on the first flight back. You make sure Parker reads him his rights this time, understood? Good. Be there soon."

When she put the phone away, Sara shook her head.

"What is it?" Victor asked.

"A suspect was brought in on a cold case of mine," Sara said. "Or, one I inherited. The state attorney is doing this new thing, assigning cold cases to those of us nearing retirement."

"You're not old enough to retire," Victor said.

She grinned at him and shook her head. "No. But I do have almost twenty-five years in, and since I'm not going to get promoted any time soon, it's about time for me to retire. I want to put this case to bed, though. And it's not going to wait."

"Nancy will," Victor said, understanding.

The smile faded from Sara's face, and she nodded. "Yes. She's not going to get any deader, so she has to wait, unfortunately."

"I understand. I'll be going in," he added.

Sara frowned. "Are you sure?"

It was his turn to smile. "Yes. I'm sure. I need to do this. I have to try and find out what's going on. I might even be able to stop any more deaths from occurring."

"You'll wait on confronting the ghost?" she asked.

"I will if I can," Victor said. "If it's any consolation, I won't be seeking a meeting with him. All I want to do is find out where he is, what he's bound to, and then try and figure out a way to catch him without putting any of the others at risk of permanent dissolution."

Sara shook her head. "Alright. Listen, I'll shoot you a text when I hit Concord, and then when I'm ready to leave again. It should only be a day or two. We'll take the guy's statement and lock him up until his attorney sweet talks his way into bail for his client, or the judge decides the suspect is going to stay locked up until the trial. Either way, I'll be talking to you soon."

"Okay," Victor said. "That sounds like a good plan to me."

"Good," she said. She reached into her pocket, took out the keys to Nancy's house and handed them to him. "Here. This way you won't have to get creative when you try to go in."

Victor smiled and tried to hide how much he had enjoyed breaking into the dead woman's house.

Together they walked back into the hotel, the two of them going their separate ways. Her car was still in its parking space when he arrived back in the lot with the key to his own rental car. Silently, he wished her the best of luck, then he got into his vehicle, started it, and left for Nancy's neighborhood.

It only took him a few minutes, and the entire time he felt as though the world had grown quieter. There didn't seem to be as many people out and about as there should have been.

Everything was unnatural.

By the time he reached Nancy's house and parked out front, Victor was feeling uncomfortable. He made sure the iron ring was on his finger, and he patted his front pocket to make certain the slim piece of iron he had packed was there as well.

Death was all around him, and it wasn't natural.

Holding onto Nancy's keys, Victor got out of the car, left it unlocked, and went to the front door. He took a deep breath and let himself into the house.

Instantly, he began to shiver. His body shook violently, and his exhalations looked more like steam pouring forth from a ruptured pipe than air from his lungs. Victor glanced around, found a closet near the door and wrenched it open. Inside of it, he found several winter coats, one of them for a man much larger than himself.

Victor pulled it on, retrieved a pair of mismatched mittens, a scarf and a wool cap, and he still felt miserably cold with the winter clothing on.

He hurried into the nearest room, a spare bedroom, and he stripped a bedspread off the mattress. Wrapping it around his shoulders, he dragged the end of it behind him as he returned to the hallway.

This, he thought, glancing at the stairs leading to the second floor, *is decidedly not good.*

He waited a minute to see if either of the ghosts would make themselves known to him, but he soon realized what he had to do.

With a sigh, Victor climbed the stairs to search for Nancy and the dead man.

He found them as soon as he turned and looked down the second-floor hallway.

And they weren't alone.

Victor had never seen so many ghosts in a single place before, and he was sure he wasn't looking at all of them.

"What happened?" he asked when he saw Nancy.

"My dream is getting stranger," she answered, "and I still can't wake up."

"We won't wake up," a voice said from behind Victor, and he twisted around to see who the speaker was.

A tall, elderly gentleman with a proud, military bearing, stood in a pair of slippers, slacks, and a polo shirt that he wore like a uniform.

"She doesn't realize we're dead," the older ghost continued. "I haven't the heart to inform her. I'm sure she'll figure it out soon enough."

"Who are you?" Victor asked.

"Bill," the dead man said. "And you are?"

"Victor."

"A pleasure, I suppose," Bill said. "This is a rather strange situation here, Victor. I'm curious, why are you here? The rest of us are dead. All killed by the boy. At least that's what I've been able to gather. We've a few among us who aren't quite sure what's going on. Much like our hostess."

"How do you know what's going on?" Victor shook his head in surprise. "I don't get it."

Bill smiled grimly. "I went through a few shocks and frights in my life, Victor. One more when I died didn't mean much of anything. And as for how I know, well, I asked. I didn't believe in ghosts when I was alive, but I suppose I don't have much of a choice about that now, do I?"

"No," Victor affirmed. "Do you know where the boy is?"

Bill shook his head. "Close by. I know that much. He makes us stay here."

"How can he *make* you?" Victor asked.

Bill shrugged. "All I know is that he said stay here, and I haven't been able to leave this property. I've tried."

"What happened?" Victor asked.

"You ever see those stupid mimes?" Bill asked. "You know, the ones who pretend they're stuck in an invisible box?"

Victor nodded.

"Just like that. I imagine that I looked fairly idiotic," Bill continued, "and I went all around the property, trying to find a way out. It's like we're in the brig. We don't have any choice. We're here until he tells us we can go."

"I need a favor from you, Bill," Victor said after a moment.

The dead man waited with an interested expression.

"Can you ask around, about where the boy might be staying?" Victor asked.

"I already have," Bill replied, a frown on his face. "First thing I did.

I hoped to get a jump on him somehow. No luck though. Anything else I can do for you?"

"Keep an eye out for the boy," Victor said after a moment. "See if you can find where he goes after he's here."

"You know that means you have to wait until he brings back another spirit?" Bill's expression was heard.

"Yes," Victor said. "I know."

"Wanted to make sure of that," Bill continued. "I didn't want it coming as a surprise."

"No," Victor said in a low voice, "death is part of the business at this point. I'm trying to keep the body count as low as possible."

Bill nodded his agreement. "Sounds about right, Victor. What'll you do now?"

"Get outside where it's warm," Victor said, "and try to see if I can find where he's hiding before he kills anyone else."

"Best of luck, son," Bill said.

"Thanks," Victor said, and still shivering, he hurried down the stairs and out of the house.

Once outside, he stripped off the extra layers and sat down on the curb. He fought the urge to vomit, for the sheer number of the dead within the house was terrifying.

I need to find this boy, Victor thought, a sense of desperation building within him. *There are too many bodies at his feet. And I wonder if he's even close to being done.*

Victor looked around the strangely quiet houses and realized he couldn't do it alone, and he couldn't wait for Sara.

He took his phone out of his pocket and called Tom.

CHAPTER 25

INFORMATION ACCESSED

The ringtone was a sharp, harsh sound that caught Stefan's attention and woke him from his half-daze in front of the monitors.

It was the boy's phone, and Stefan had been surprised earlier to find it was unlocked.

Picking the cellphone up, Stefan saw that the ID read, *Home*, and he answered the call.

"Tom?" a man asked, worry and concern in his voice.

The boy's father, Stefan thought and repressed a pang of jealousy. Ivan Denisovich had never sounded worried or concerned when he had called for Stefan. Only disappointed.

"I'm afraid not," Stefan said cheerfully, reclining in his chair. "Who's this?"

"I'm his father," the man answered. "Where's my son?"

"Playing with things he shouldn't," Stefan replied. "Or, rather, that's what landed him here. I suppose."

"And where's here?" the man demanded.

"Well, let's have your name first, alright?" Stefan asked, picking up the boy's prosthetic.

"Victor," the man said tightly. "Victor Daniels."

Stefan stiffened and put the arm down. He remembered the name and hesitated before he said, "Do you know why your son's here, Mr. Daniels?"

"Where's here?" Victor asked again, his voice harsh.

"With me," Stefan replied. "He's here since you're not asking why, because he tried to trespass. In fact, I think he meant to do me some harm. I've got a 9mm semi-automatic here, fully loaded. And ten, yes, ten claymore mines. I'm impressed. Even I have a hard time getting my hands on claymores. The military usually pays pretty close attention to them."

"Who," Victor hissed, "are you, and where is my son?"

"Oh, that's right, I didn't introduce myself," Stefan said, chuckling. "I'm Stefan Korzh, and your boy is here with me."

Silence greeted Stefan's statement.

He couldn't even hear the man breathing.

"Hello?" Stefan asked after a moment.

"I'm going to kill you," Victor said, and there was no anger in his voice. He sounded matter of fact as if he was telling a friend he was going down to the store for a loaf of bread. "It will be quick. And it will be painless. I'm not an animal. Not anymore. But you're going to die, and I'm going to be the one who kills you."

Stefan had been threatened many times in his life, and often by individuals who were more than capable of killing him.

But he had never been afraid of anyone other than his father, and even that had been tempered with time.

Victor Daniels' calm, self-assured statement was like a cold knife in the belly of Stefan's self-esteem.

"If you come anywhere near me," Stefan snapped, "I'll gut him like a fish and leave him alive for you to find."

It took him a moment to realize Victor had hung up, and that he hadn't heard Stefan's threat.

Furious, Stefan stood up, dropped the phone to the chair, and stormed out of the room.

I want to know how the boy got those damned claymores, he thought and stomped down the hall towards the boy's makeshift prison.

***

Victor's hands shook as he accessed his phone's settings and activated the app to find Tom's phone. He had installed it after Tom had lost his forearm, although he had never told the boy about it. Victor had never thought he would have to use the app, but its mere existence had helped him to rest when he was worried about the boy.

Swallowing dryly, Victor held the phone in both hands and waited for the information to come through.

***

A sharp, heavy bang snapped Tom out of a dreamless sleep and set his heart racing.

"You awake?" Korzh demanded.

"I am now," Tom replied.

"Where did you get the claymores?" Korzh asked.

Tom smiled. "A couple of punks. They got them, and I bought them."

"Who are they?" Korzh sounded enraged, and Tom knew he should be frightened, but he wasn't.

"I don't know them, not really," Tom answered. "And I don't think they're around. Bontoc scared them."

"He's dead, how can he," Korzh began, but then his voice trailed off.

Now you know how, Tom thought. *And you're wondering if he can get in here. Let's hope the answer to that question is 'yes'.*

Tom waited for Korzh to speak again, but there was nothing. It took him a moment to realize Korzh had left.

Settling back against the wall, the question Tom didn't want to ask made itself known again.

Why hadn't Bontoc done anything to help me?

The dead man hadn't been so far from him that he wouldn't have noticed something going wrong. Bontoc couldn't have missed Tom's sudden disappearance, or of Korzh hauling his unconscious body away.

A miserable, feeling of betrayal wrapped itself around Tom's stomach and squeezed. He knew Bontoc hated Korzh, and that he wanted the man dead.

But what if I was only bait? Tom wondered. *What if I was used to draw Korzh out? And does Bontoc even care what happens to me?*

Tom knew the answer, and he felt ashamed. Not from his own naïve belief in Bontoc, but from the understanding that he had let Victor down.

And that he was going to die without saying goodbye to the man who had been the best father he had known.

CHAPTER 26

At Any Time and Soon

"Daughter."

The sound of her father's voice snapped Ariana out of her sleep, and she fought the urge to leap out of bed.

Around her, the bedroom was dark, even the ever-present light on her alarm clock was absent.

Ivan Denisovich was in her room.

"Hello, father," she said, sitting up and wrapping her blanket around her.

"Are you cold?" he asked, a hint of a smile in his voice.

"Of course, I am," Ariana said, forcing a laugh. "You're dead. That tends to bring the temperature down in any enclosed space."

"Ah," her father said with a pleased sigh. "The little things. You were always aware of them, my dear daughter. Much more so than Stefan. At times, it was as though I was speaking to the proverbial brick wall."

And still you stayed with him and your wife, Ariana thought. Aloud she stated, "He may be a slow learner, father, but when it sticks, it sticks."

Ivan Denisovich chuckled. "Truer words were never spoken. At least in the case of your half-brother. Now, I have managed to speak with Anne Le Morte."

"Is all well with her?" Ariana then added in a false tone of hope, "Has she taken care of Stefan for you?"

"Alas," her dead father said. "There is no such luck. But she is expecting you, and she knows to not harm you. The consequences would be severe."

Ariana nodded. "I would like to leave in the morning. Is this acceptable?"

"It is," Ivan Denisovich said, and there was an unmistakable note of pride in his voice. "Your respect is a marvel, and it always pleases me. Leave as soon as you can. She will be waiting for you. Together, you will seek out your half-brother and attend to him."

"And when that is done," Ariana said. "May I come once more to your home?"

"Your home as well," her father said. "And yes. I insist. I will see you when the task is complete."

"Thank you, father," Ariana whispered.

A heartbeat later, the alarm clock returned to life, 12:00 flashing in red.

Ariana got out of bed and went to her closet to gather clothes. She wouldn't be able to sleep, not with the knowledge that her father had cleared the path for her towards her half-brother.

Heading towards the bathroom to shower, Ariana's focus began to sharpen.

It was time to hunt down Stefan and finally kill him.

CHAPTER 27

FURY AND WRATH UNITED

Victor stood in his own kitchen and tried to calm his racing thoughts.

The house was empty, which he had expected.

But the car was gone, and that had surprised him.

There was no note, no hint as to where the boy might have gone. The only clue was the basic information the app gave Victor as to the location of the phone.

And he could only hope that Tom and the phone were still in the same place.

Victor thought about what he could do against Stefan Korzh, and he realized there wasn't much. He could battle a ghost with iron, and he could trap them as well. But in regards to a weapon that would be successful against Stefan, a man Victor knew to be deadly, he doubted he had anything lethal.

I don't need lethal. Not right now, Victor thought. *No, I only need to save Tom. After that, well, then I can find something to finish the job. But Tom is my priority.*

Victor left the kitchen and descended the stairs into the basement. He went to the small work area where he had a sawed-off, double-barrel shotgun clamped down in a small, table-top vise. For several days prior to his trip, he had worked on smoothing out the rough edges where the barrels had been cut short. Tom had joked about removing the stock of the weapon, leaving only a rough grip.

Listen, Tom had said, laughing, *you aren't going for aim with a sawed-off, right? At least with the stock gone, you can hide it under a jacket.*

Victor picked up the hacksaw he had used on the barrels and in a matter of minutes cut the stock away. He used a rough piece of sandpaper to get rid of the worst of the edges. The weapon was lighter, and as he swung it several times in different directions, Victor realized how quickly he could bring the gun to bear on a target.

And what if he has some of the dead guarding his home? Victor wondered.

He hesitated for a moment, and then thought, *Rock-salt. It'll stop the dead and hurt anyone still alive. And I need to know where Tom is. What he's done with him.*

Victor shuddered, regained control of himself and thought, *If Korzh is dead, I might not find Tom. He might be hidden somewhere.*

Korzh needs to be alive.

He stuffed his pockets with extra rounds of rock-salt, then he picked up a metal box-cutter. Victor slid the blade out and saw it was new, then he closed it and added it to an already bulging pocket.

Just because it's not lethal, Victor thought, climbing the stairs back to the main floor, *doesn't mean it isn't going to hurt.*

And he had every intention of making Stefan Korzh hurt.

CHAPTER 28:
SEEING THE TRAP

The knock on the door caught her by surprise.

"Mrs. Simon?" a man asked. "Mrs. Simon, are you alright?"

Leanne pushed herself up and out of the chair, limped to the front door and pitched her voice low and hoarse, replying, "Yes."

"It's Ron, Mrs. Simon, your mailman," the man said, relief in his voice. "Are you alright?"

Leanne forced herself to cough and said, "Sick."

"Do you need a doctor?" he asked.

Go away! Leanne wanted to scream, but she was weaker than she expected.

And a mailman would certainly be missed.

"No, thank you," she said, coughing again.

"Alright," he said after a moment. "Well, the mail is here. You call on down to the office if you need anything. We'll take care of it."

She thanked the man again and listened as he walked heavily to the street. A moment later the roar of an engine filled the air, and she shook her head at her own stupidity.

He drove up here! I'm a damned fool for not hearing that. She was bitter as she returned to the seat, easing herself down into it. Her stomach rumbled, but she lacked the desire to go into the kitchen and cut a bit of flesh from the old woman, Mrs. Simon, who was quartered and shoved into the refrigerator to help the meat stay fresh.

I need a way out of here, she thought morosely. *And I can't get back the way I came. Not enough money in here to let me even take a bus back to Louisiana.*

I'm trapped.

The realization caused frustration to burn within her, and she gripped the arms of the chair until her fingers hurt. Leanne squeezed her eyes closed and focused on what she needed to do.

I must escape from New Hampshire, she thought, *if I am to have my vengeance on Victor Daniels. And for that to occur, I need strength, and a means to travel.*

With sheer force of will, Leanne cleared her mind and let her thoughts roll out into darkness. Then, quite suddenly, a sound came back to her. A voice speaking in a foreign tongue.

German? she thought, opening her eyes.

Bah, the language doesn't matter, Leanne decided. *Whoever was speaking it is powerful, and nearby. I might be able to use them to find Victor.*

She stood up, wavered for a moment, and waited until she was sure of her balance.

I will need my strength, Leanne thought, and she went into the kitchen. For several minutes she rummaged around the well-cared-for room, selecting the pans and seasoning she needed. Then, satisfied that all was ready, she turned her attention to the refrigerator. When she opened its door, the rank, iron scent of blood assailed her nose, and Leanne smiled as she leaned forward and decided which piece of Mrs. Simon she would feast upon.

CHAPTER 29

A FINE BLEND

Fury, panic, and trepidation simmered within Stefan Korzh's heart, and behind it all he struggled to retain control.

He walked the perimeter of his compound, seeking out any sort of disturbance in the fencing, anything that showed he wasn't as safe as he thought.

Stefan came to a stop, and his heart skipped several beats.

The PVC piping he had filled with salt near a No Trespassing sign was pulled up and broken.

He licked his lips nervously, then broke into a jog, eye darting from the PVC to the fence and beyond.

Somewhere, Anne Le Morte's caretaker watched him, he was sure of it.

And he was just as certain that it had been the woman, under Anne's guidance, who had destroyed his protective barrier.

Don't forget about Bontoc, Stefan thought, and he reached up and adjusted the patch over his empty eye socket.

He reached the closed gate, and a new fear sprang up within him.

If they knew about the salt, he thought, *did they know about the truck?*

For a split second, he considered going back and checking on the boy, of going back and making sure everything was locked.

But it wouldn't matter if they had gotten to his truck.

Stefan ripped open the gate and sprinted down the road.

***

"Not yet," Anne said in French, and Grace lowered her shotgun.

"The other one is not here yet," Anne continued. "And it would be best to have the job done all at once."

"I was only going to wound him," Grace sulked.

Bontoc chuckled. "With that man, it will be best to kill him with a single blow, or at least break his back so he cannot flee. I underestimated him, and look where I am. It is a good thing he does not collect heads, or mine would be on his wall."

There was silence for a moment, then Bontoc asked, "Where is he going?"

"To his truck," Grace replied.

"Ah," Bontoc said. "Has something happened to it?"

Grace smirked and said no more.

***

Stefan had not kept up with his cardio, and he suffered accordingly.

By the time he reached his pickup, he had already vomited twice.

With the bitter taste of bile in his mouth, he came to a staggering halt and stared with pure hatred at his truck.

Or what was left of it.

The tires hung in black ribbons from the rims and the entire area stank of gasoline. Near the driver's side door lay the distributor cap and various filters were scattered about. The crankcase was open and covered in sand, and there was a message scratched into the side of the truck in French, and Stefan translated it.

My dear friend, Mr. Stefan Korzh. It is good, is it not?

No, Stefan fumed, *it is not good, you foul witch.*

He drew his pistol and fired several rounds into the words.

I can't wait to destroy you.

CHAPTER 30:
ON THE WIND

Three quick shots caught Victor's attention and caused him to stop.

The sounds had come from up around a slight bend in the road the GPS had him following.

His mouth went dry with fear, and he wondered if Stefan Korzh had killed Tom. If the man had somehow known that Victor was on his way.

No, Victor thought, refusing to surrender to the fear. *He can't know.*

Victor moved forward again, keeping to the side of the road, the shotgun bouncing around the inside of his coat, his palms slick with a cold sweat. The idea of finding Tom's corpse kept leaping forward, and Victor battered it back. Tom wouldn't die at Stefan Korzh's hands.

Victor rounded the corner and saw a truck parked on the side of the road, and it had been vandalized. A man stood beside it, a pistol in his hand and a look of pure rage on his face.

As Victor drew nearer, the man seemed to notice him for the first time.

The gun remained at his side, but Victor came to a stop and held his hands up to show he was unarmed.

"This is private property," the stranger said, adjusting the black patch over his left eye.

And as the words left his mouth, Victor stiffened.

He recognized the voice.

It was Stefan Korzh.

Victor's own words came out remarkably smooth and unaffected.

"I'm sorry," Victor said, smiling. "I was out for a walk. I'm new to the area. I think I got turned around. I live about half a mile up on Danvers Road."

"You're about three miles too far," Stefan replied. He eyed Victor for a moment, hesitated as if he knew who Victor was, and then holstered his pistol with a small shake of his head. "Turn around. Follow the road until it ends, then turn left. You'll be home soon enough. And remember, this is private property."

"I will," Victor said, "and thanks."

Stefan nodded, turned back to the car, and Victor drew the shotgun.

The weapon roared, and the rock-salt slammed into Stefan's right arm. Korzh screamed in rage as he stumbled back, his arm hanging limply as he struggled to draw the pistol with his left.

"Where's my son?" Victor asked, reloading the weapon and firing again. The shot missed and Stefan drew the pistol with his left.

Victor dropped down to one knee as Stefan fired off several rounds that struck the road around Victor.

With the heat of the spent shell burning his fingertips, Victor glared at Stefan and reloaded again.

As Stefan brought the pistol up with his left hand, Victor fired again, and while the pattern from the rock-salt was wide, enough struck Korzh in the face to spin the man around.

"Where is he?" Victor demanded, and as he went to reload again, something struck him from behind, sending him sprawling onto the road, the shotgun clattering off to one side.

Victor didn't see what had attacked him, but Stefan did, and the man wore a mixed expression of anger and fear.

Victor struggled to get up, but a blow to the back of the head sent him into darkness.

***

Stefan stared at the mangled ghost which straddled the prostrate form of Victor Daniels, the man who had attacked him.

I didn't recognize him! He thought, furious with himself as he kept his eye on Bontoc. *Damn Anne Le Morte and her games!*

The sting of the minor wounds inflicted by the rock-salt formed a dull-background for the fear that surged through him.

Bontoc, bearing all the grisly wounds Stefan had inflicted upon him in their final battle, smiled at him.

"Stefan Korzh," Bontoc said, grinning at him. "Do you remember me?"

With his right arm still numb from the impact of the salt-rounds, Stefan reluctantly dropped his pistol and took a small piece of iron out of his pocket, closing his fist tightly around it.

Bontoc nodded. "Yes. Strange that such a minor item as iron might lay me low now."

The dead man chuckled. "Stranger still that one such as you were able to defeat me."

"Why are you here?" Stefan demanded, glancing around to make certain no one was sneaking up on him.

"There is still a bounty on your head," Bontoc said, his grin widening. "I intend to collect it."

"You're dead," Stefan stated.

The dead man shrugged.

The roar of another shotgun cut off Stefan's next statement, and Bontoc vanished.

From the tree-line, a figure emerged.

Recognition blazed in Stefan's mind, and he turned and fled.

Behind him, his half-sister stepped onto the road.

Stefan ran as hard and as fast as he could. His pain and fear were cast aside, replaced by the sheer will that had driven him for years. He had assessed the situation in an instant.

Bontoc could be beaten back by a piece of iron.

Ariana would pick him apart with whatever firearms she carried, and Stefan wouldn't be able to defend himself.

Flight was the best option.

He dry-heaved as he ran, but he refused to allow himself to slow down. Instead, he thrust the iron back into his pocket and dropped pieces of equipment as he went. With each slight piece of weight cast aside, the faster he felt he could run.

Soon the gate of his compound could be seen, as could another figure. An entirely human figure.

A shotgun was raised up, and Anne Le Morte's caretaker fired at him.

The shot was wide, and as the woman struggled to reload, Stefan was on her. Her eyes widened with fear as he wrenched the shotgun out of her hands, reversed it and used the butt of the weapon to knock her down. The woman twisted as she fell, landing on her hands and springing up faster than Stefan thought she could.

With a snarl, she attacked, and while she lacked finesse and skill, she made up for it with an impressive fury. Her fists were a blur, almost too fast for Stefan to block with the large and clumsy shotgun.

But he did turn them aside and with each he heard fingers break. Her expression never changed, even as her right forearm broke. She tried a kick and for a moment, she was off balance, giving Stefan the opening he needed.

Swinging the shotgun with all the grace of a professional golfer, Stefan caught her in the stomach. The power of the blow lifted her up off her feet and for a moment she seemed to hang in the air, then she plummeted down.

She sprawled backward onto the pavement, dazed, and before she could get up, Stefan allowed his rage to flow.

He broke the thick stock of the shotgun as he smashed it in her skull, bits of bone and brain and blood spraying up into his face. In the distance, he heard an enraged shriek and realized that Anne Le Morte knew her caretaker was dead.

Dropping the useless weapon, Stefan sprinted across the pavement, and as he neared the entrance to the warehouse, Bontoc emerged. Stefan retrieved his piece of iron.

The ghost seemed surprised to see Stefan, and as he opened his mouth, Stefan drove his fist through the ghost.

In seconds, Stefan was back in the safety of the warehouse, staggering toward the other vehicle he owned. The battered Ford Taurus had a full tank of gas, and his emergency bag, packed with spare weapons, cash, and keys to a safe house, was in the trunk.

Stefan climbed in, turned the car over and hit the remote that controlled not only a door at the far end of the warehouse, but a small set of charges on a length of the fence near an access road. There was a slight shudder as the vibration of the demolition of the fence rippled through the building.

Off to his right, Stefan saw Bontoc appear in the open doorway to his quarters.

Stefan slammed the car into gear, stomped on the gas, and fled his home, abandoning the warehouse to the dead.

CHAPTER 31:
ON THE ROAD

Stefan had vanished around the curve of the road before Ariana had been able to switch from her shotgun to the AR-15 she had brought with her. She had let him go, knowing that the only place he could run to was the warehouse, and she could burn him out, if necessary.

There's no place for you to go, Stefan, she thought. *This is the only road.*

Ariana shifted her focus to the unconscious form of Victor Daniels, who lay in a heap on the cracked pavement of the road. She wasn't sure what happened, but when she had neared the tree line, Ariana had seen Bontoc standing over Victor and conversing with her half-brother.

With her shotgun reloaded and on the ground beside her, Ariana gingerly rolled Victor over and saw he had slight abrasions on his forehead, and his nose was swollen, although not necessarily broken.

She shook her head, reached down with her right hand, and slapped him gently on either cheek. When he didn't respond, Ariana increased the force of the blows until his eyelids fluttered and he awoke.

She helped him as he scrambled into a sitting position and he looked around in a daze.

"Ariana?" he asked, confused.

"Of course," she said. "What are you doing here?"

"Stefan has my son." Victor got to his feet, weaving like a drunk. She reached out a hand and steadied him.

"How do you know?" Ariana asked, unable to mask her surprise.

"He told me," Victor said. "When I called Tom. Stefan answered."

"Did he tell you to come here?"

Victor shook his head. "GPS on Tom's phone."

He looked around, picked up his own shotgun and reloaded it before he began to stumble and stagger along the road. Ariana took her shotgun and easily kept pace with him.

Victor spat out a wad of bloody spit and apologized. A moment later he asked, "Why are you here? Never mind. Stupid question. How did you find this place?"

"Good old-fashioned research," she replied. "Then I talked with Ivan Denisovich about calling Anne Le Morte off so I could go in after Stefan."

She watched Victor as he managed to reload his shotgun, despite the obvious head trauma he was suffering from.

"Maybe you should let me go ahead," Ariana said as gently as possible.

Victor shook his head, winced, and said, "My son."

Ariana nodded in reply and let the matter drop. Instead, she focused on the problem of forcing her half-brother out of his fortress if Tom Daniels really was a prisoner. She had no doubt that Stefan would use the boy as leverage.

A rattle of small explosives cut off her thoughts, and she had to reach out and restrain Victor from running forward.

His eyes were wild with hate and fear as he spun around on her.

"Victor!" she snapped. "Get a grip, or you're going to put Tom in even greater danger."

She heard the man grind his teeth together, the muscles on his jaw standing out as he nodded.

A squeal of tires reached her ears, and she stiffened.

"Tom," Victor whispered.

"Slow," she responded, "or you're going to crash and burn, and that won't do your boy any good."

Victor gave a short nod, and they started along the road again.

As they rounded the corner, Ariana saw the building that Stefan had been using as a home. It was an old warehouse; one that had seen better days. One of the huge garage doors was open, and a little further away a cloud of dust hung in the still air beyond a section of missing fence.

Ariana scoffed and shook her head.

He had a backup vehicle, she thought, *and an emergency way out. I bet that's an access road that cuts to some highway.*

"Who's that?" Victor asked in a low, trembling voice.

Ahead of them, a body lay in front of the open gate into the warehouse's mammoth parking lot.

"Hold on," Ariana said, and she swung her AR-15 up into position and used the ACOG scope to get a better look at the figure.

The head was beaten to a pulp, and a shotgun lay on the ground next to the corpse.

"That's not your son," Ariana said, lowering her rifle.

"Are you sure?" Victor asked.

Ariana bit her tongue to keep back a sarcastic response, and said, "I'm sure. Unless your boy has long, dirty hair of indeterminate color and has been living in the woods for a few months. No, Victor, I'm positive that's the body of Anne Le Morte's caretaker. Which means we're going to have to make certain we don't go into the woods. Not for any reason at all. I don't know how far away Anne might be hidden, but I doubt it's far enough. And with her caretaker dead, well, I don't think she's going to be in a good mood."

"Will she even notice?" Victor asked.

Ariana hesitated, then answered, "To be honest, I don't know. She might not. At least not right away."

"Well," Victor said, grunting as he shifted his shotgun from one hand to the other, "let's hope the day doesn't get any worse."

CHAPTER 32

PHYSICAL MANIFESTATIONS

Victor's stomach churned as he stepped around the corpse of Anne Le Morte's dead caretaker. He had never seen such violence done to a human in person, and a gnawing fear settled in his stomach as he realized that he could enter the warehouse and find Tom in a similar if not worse condition.

Don't, he snapped. *Don't think like that. He's going to be fine. I know that.*

But no matter how much he lied to himself, Victor didn't know that.

He limped on towards the open garage door, Ariana keeping pace with him until they were twenty or so feet from the building.

"Stop, Victor," she said, and there was a cold authority to her voice. Her brutal professionalism had taken control, and Victor did as she said.

He watched as she double checked the AR-15, flipped the safety off and said, "I'm going to take the lead. If I tell you to stop, you stop. No questions. Understood?"

"Yes," Victor said, gritting his teeth. His head throbbed and ached, and he was certain he was at least mildly concussed. He got a better grip on his shotgun and followed Ariana's lead the rest of the distance into the dim warehouse.

His eyes adjusted quickly, and he saw a small cluster of offices in the huge building's center. Ariana approached a small door of the first office cautiously and glanced back, waving Victor off to the left, behind her. When he had done so, she dropped to a crouch, reached out with her left hand, and twisted the doorknob. She shoved the door in and brought her hand swiftly back up to the rifle.

After several seconds, she straightened up and lowered her weapons slightly.

"Come on," she said, crossing the threshold.

Victor nodded, not worrying about traps.

He was concerned only with finding Tom.

"Be careful," Ariana said as they entered the small cluster of rooms, "Stefan isn't here, but he may have left behind a trap or two."

Again, fear for Tom's safety sprang up and threatened to choke him, and Victor shoved it down.

"There," Ariana said, pointing towards a tall box.

"The packing crate?" Victor asked.

She shook her head, strode forward, and pressed a small button on a panel that Victor hadn't seen.

"Tom?" she asked.

There was a click, and a moment later Tom answered tiredly, "Yeah. Who's this?"

Ariana glanced over to Victor, but he couldn't speak.

"Step back from the door, if you can," she said.

"No can do," Tom said. "But I can turn away from it."

"Good enough," she said.

Ariana nodded to Victor and said, "Use the butt of your shotgun, right here where the padlock loops through the eye. Don't try and break the lock. Focus on ripping the screws out of the wood. Stefan built this quick, otherwise, we would need a saws-all to get Tom out of there."

"Alright," Victor said, wishing he had brought his lock-picking tools with him.

Doesn't matter, he thought, and with several blows, he smashed the lock and hardware out of the improvised prison.

As he stepped back and caught his breath, Ariana pulled the door backward and the pale light of the office shined down upon Tom.

The boy looked tired and exceptionally small without his prosthetic, but he was alive.

"You're an idiot," Victor whispered.

Tom nodded, wiped tears from his eyes and stood up. "I'm sorry."

The young man walked out of the cell and embraced Victor, and once more, he was reminded of how strong Tom was.

After a moment, Tom pulled back and said, "You're Ariana."

"Yes, I am," she said, extending her hand.

Tom shook it. "Nice AR."

The woman grinned and said, "Thank you."

"Where's your prosthetic?" Victor asked.

"I wish I knew," Tom answered. "He must have locked it up. Probably in a lead-lined box, or in salt. He must have figured out Bontoc was in the ring."

"Probably," Victor agreed. "He moves fast. Korzh may even have had it prepped to go."

"We better find it then," Ariana said. "And we should do it quickly. Anne's going to figure out something's wrong sooner or later, and I would really like to not be here when that occurs."

Tom's face paled at the mention of Anne Le Morte, and he nodded his agreement.

Hurriedly, they moved through the rooms, pausing only once to stare at the impressive surveillance system Stefan had set up. A few minutes later, Ariana called out from a small room, "Here!"

Victor and Tom found her standing by a small bed, on which was a backpack, claymore mines, and Tom's arm.

But the ring was gone.

"Did he take it with him?" Tom asked anxiously, looking around the bed and under it.

"Maybe," Ariana said. "Especially if he figured out Bontoc was attached to it. I'm just curious as to where the hell Stefan got claymore mines. Those are hard for me to get a hold of."

Victor noticed color rise to Tom's cheeks.

"Tom," Victor said, "are those yours?"

His son nodded.

Ariana's eyes widened with appreciation. "Holy crap, kid. Were you going to blow this place up?"

"That was the plan," Tom confessed.

Ariana laughed. "That is an awesome plan."

"Ariana," Victor started.

She shook her head. "No, seriously. We're miles away from civilization. I can take the C4 out of the claymores, rig some other stuff together and blow whatever haunted items are still around to kingdom come."

Victor wanted to disagree but discovered that she was right.

He looked at Tom and said, "I'm not going to ask where you got the claymores. Or how you managed to find someone who would sell them to you. We will, however, have a lengthy discussion about stupid decisions, like going after Stefan Korzh by yourself."

Tom didn't argue.

Victor sighed. "Okay. I need your help in that big brother room Korzh had set up."

Both Tom and Ariana looked at him inquisitively, and Victor smiled coldly.

"I'm guessing a control freak like Stefan will have kept detailed records of who he sold haunted items to and what those items were." Victor rubbed at the pain in his head before he continued. "And I'm sure that most of the dead can be identified by Moran and Moran, so long as there isn't another auction in the near future."

"And you'll track them down?" Tom asked.

Victor shook his head. "We'll track them down. I'll homeschool you, if you want, that way I won't have to leave you behind, and we won't risk anyone being injured or killed by the others."

"Good," Tom said softly.

"Will this take long?" Victor asked.

"A little bit," Ariana said with a feral grin. "You can't rush when you're working with explosives."

"True," Victor admitted. "I only ask because there's a ghost on a killing spree."

"Get what you need and take off," Ariana said. "I have your number. If I find anything else, I'll let you know. And I want to talk to you about Stefan as well."

Victor nodded.

"Come on," he said to Tom, and the two of them exited the room, leaving Ariana to examine the claymores.

***

She had said her goodbyes to both Victor and Tom, and when she was certain they were gone, she constructed a small but efficient timer for the bomb she had built.

Ariana walked close to the bomb where a small, but thick circle of salt lay on the battered and stained concrete floor. Crouching down beside the circle, Ariana withdrew a matchbox from her pocket. The item was made of lead encased in steel, and it served as an effective prison, when necessary.

Ariana held it out over the circle, just an inch or so above the floor, and opened it.

The aluminum ring fell and struck heavily for such a light piece of metal.

Bontoc appeared a moment later, a sour expression on his disfigured face.

"What is the meaning of this, Ariana?" he demanded.

She straightened up and moved back, out of arm's reach. Ariana wasn't certain if the ghost would find a way through the salt, or if some errant breeze would destroy the ring, but she wasn't taking any chances.

"You're not stupid," she replied, placing the matchbox back in her pocket. "Sociopathic, but definitely not stupid. You tell me why I'm doing this."

The feigned outrage on his face vanished, and he smiled, which, she decided was worse than his glare.

"You saw me strike down Victor," the dead man said.

She nodded. "Why?"

"He might have harmed your brother," Bontoc started.

"Half-brother," she interrupted, correcting him.

He bowed his head slightly. "Half-brother. It is not up to Victor Daniels to inflict any punishment upon Stefan Korzh. That honor is reserved for Anne Le Morte and me."

"Funny," Ariana said, a cold feeling creeping up along her spine. "Dear old Dad told me that I could take care of Stefan."

Bontoc smirked and remained silent. But his eyes flickered to the open garage behind her.

Ariana didn't look away from the dead man.

"I hope you're not expecting Anne," Ariana said. "Or her caretaker. Stefan beat the woman to death with her own shotgun. Right before he left."

"They didn't stop him?" the surprise in his voice held a tinge of rage.

She shook her head. "In fact, I expect Anne will shortly figure out what happened. Or at least suspect what happened."

"He can't have gotten away completely," Bontoc said with a growl. "That isn't how this is supposed to go."

The dead man's voice was rising, fury appearing on his face.

"He is supposed to die," Bontoc snapped.

"Yup," Ariana agreed. "He tends to not do that, however."

"I'm going to kill him," Bontoc hissed. "He's going to die. Quickly, but I will be the one to do it!"

Ariana grinned. "No. I don't think so."

"Silence!" Bontoc spat.

"No, that's not going to happen either."

"You're going to be dead soon, too," the ghost said, his voice becoming low and dangerous.

"You won't have anything to do with it," Ariana said, walking over to the timer for the bomb.

"You're wrong!" The dead man threw himself towards her, but the power of the salt stopped him, standing him upright as if he were caged.

Ariana blinked, then grinned.

"You won't be smirking much longer," Bontoc said, his voice a low guttural growl. "You'll be bound. As will your brother, and we shall deliver unto your father."

Ariana straightened up, the smile indeed gone from her face.

Bontoc blinked, a look of fear appearing for a moment in his eyes.

"What did you say?" she asked softly.

"Nothing," was the dead man's hurried response.

"Who is going to bind me?" Her voice was tight. "Is it you?"

The ghost hesitated, then shook his head. "I don't have that kind of strength. To bind another."

"No," Ariana said, letting the thought roll around in her head. "But Anne Le Morte does. What is she going to bind me to?"

The dead man seemed to weigh his options, glanced at her and answered, "There is a small set of nesting dolls."

Ariana held up her hand to stop Bontoc from saying any more.

She knew what he spoke of.

"Those nesting dolls," Ariana said, choosing her words carefully. "Are they of a blue queen, with a crown of ice and fire?"

The dead man nodded.

She let out a bitter laugh and held back her tears only through force of will.

"I know those dolls," Ariana said. "They were my mother's. I looked for them when she died. I couldn't find them."

"Your father," Bontoc said, "he made certain Anne Le Morte was in the house when the strangling woman slew your mother. Your mother is bound to them as well."

"Is she?" Ariana's voice was hardly more than a whisper.

The dead man nodded, a note of confidence returning to his voice. "I know where they are."

"I'm sure you do," Ariana said, and she smiled at him. "Tell me, if you would, why am I to be bound to the dolls?"

"Your father, he wants his family together," Bontoc said. "He wants all of you together. And when you and your brother have been brought back into the fold, you will be delivered to him. The key awaits, and the dolls will be placed in the room with him, where he will join you. A family, as you were all, always meant to be."

"Yes," Ariana said, nodding. "I can see the logic in that."

"Are you angry with me?" Bontoc asked, smiling.

"Not at all," she said, walking past him to her home-made bomb. Ariana picked up the old analog alarm clock she had found among Stefan's possessions. None of the components for her bomb required electronics. A simple mix of chemicals and the clock to set off an explosion to trigger the C4.

"What are you doing?" Bontoc asked.

"Not being angry," she replied, winding the clock.

"Then what are you doing?!" he demanded, fear in his voice.

"Tidying up," Ariana answered. The ticking of the clock was loud and reassuring. "I'm sure I'll see you in Hell."

Bontoc's screams filled her ears as she walked out of the warehouse.

She had no need to run.

And Bontoc, she thought. *Well, he can't.*

Ariana adjusted her weapons, wondering how best to destroy her father.

CHAPTER 33

LOATHING

Stefan stood beside his car in the parking lot of a small convenience store, drinking a bottle of water and idly shaking a container of Advil in his free hand.

A distant explosion shook the windows of the store and sent the employees and customers running out to see what it was.

Stefan knew what it was.

They blew up my warehouse, he thought, anger and hatred merging together and spreading through him. *They destroyed it all.*

He watched the smoke rise in the distance while nearly everyone from the store recorded the scene on their phones. Stefan resisted the urge to kill them all and help slake his fury. Instead, he finished his water and got into his car. For a short time, he stared at the wall of the store, his mind mulling over what little information there was to process.

My half-sister is helping Victor Daniels, he thought, rubbing at his chin. *Daniels' son brought explosives. One of them knew enough to set up a bomb, and one without electronics because otherwise the ghost of the hunter would have made it inoperable. And then, that explosion. That's not just the C4.*

Stefan shook his head and started the car.

No, he thought, backing the vehicle up and exiting the parking lot. *That's the result of all of the haunted items being destroyed at once.*

A small part of him was pleased that the items were gone.

But that was only a small part.

Furious at being driven from his home, Stefan drove towards his safe house and let his mind roam over the various options for revenge that remained open to him.

***

Anne Le Morte lay on her back as the ground shook beneath the cloth and porcelain doll that she possessed. For hours, she had lain like a newborn babe, swaddled in an old shirt and placed at the far end of the small hovel her caretaker had erected.

With the explosion, Anne realized something.

She is dead, the ghost thought. *I must find another.*

Her caretaker's death left Anne Le Morte unfazed. There had been others before the woman, and there would be more after her. This, she knew, was as certain as the sun rising in the morning and setting in the evening.

Anne went to free herself from the cloth and found that she could not. She struggled against it, but to no avail. The caretaker had made it too secure. Angry, she let out an enraged scream, and while the flimsy walls of the hovel shook, they were too well-secured.

Her caretaker had made certain Anne would be safe until the woman's return.

But she won't be returning! Anne fumed. *The stupid cow was slain and has trapped me!*

Anne forced her mind to calm itself and let her senses open. She searched for signs of civilization, of people walking or driving. But her range was limited, and there was nothing.

No houses. No shops. Not even a person walking along the slim game trails she had followed.

Anne Le Morte was alone and trapped.

With a furious and silent snarl, Anne settled her mind and waited.

Soon, she thought, *someone will pass by, and I will convince them to help, as I have convinced all the others.*

The idea of her future success pleased her, and Anne sang softly to herself, hoping her stay in the hovel wouldn't be for long.

Ivan Denisovich's children still needed to be slain.

CHAPTER 34

HOME AND STRUGGLING

Victor slumped in his chair in the study. Tom was asleep, his face drawn and pale.

Their discussion had been short and brief with Victor doing most of the talking. He did not lay down ironclad rules as his own father had done, nor did he attempt to chalk Tom's actions up to the hubris of youth.

Tom wouldn't be hunting on his own, and he hadn't tried to defend his actions.

Victor hadn't punished him.

Being held as a prisoner by the man who had killed his parents had been punishment enough.

Victor's phone rang, and he answered it.

"Hello?" he asked.

"Victor," Shane said. "You found him."

"I did," Victor answered. He had left a message for the other man earlier.

"Was it bad?" Shane asked.

"Bad enough," Victor answered. He gave Shane a quick synopsis, and the other man uttered several choice words. When he finished, Victor asked, "How are things up there?"

"Strange," Shane answered. "The dead are in an uproar about something, but they won't tell me. I don't know if it's just this area, or if it's on a wider scale, but they're acting like trouble is on its way, even though they don't know what that trouble is."

"I'm sorry to hear that," Victor said.

"Me too," Shane said. Victor heard the click of a lighter, a long exhale, and then Shane continued. "Anyway, I'm glad you have him. What are you two doing now?"

"He's asleep in a chair, and I'm going to try and get some rest," Victor answered. "We've got a problem in another town that needs to be taken care of."

"You're not leaving him alone again?" Shane asked.

"No," Victor said. "Not at all."

"Good," Shane said. "Listen, do me a favor, Victor, call or text me when you get to wherever it is you're going. I want to know you two are okay."

Victor chuckled and said, "I will."

They ended the call, and Victor looked at Tom. The boy was still asleep, and Victor knew he needed to be as well.

Closing his eyes, Victor got comfortable in his chair, not willing to leave the child alone just yet.

***

Leanne contemplated calling for a cab, but a paranoia grew within her as she considered such an act.

What if this woman called for cabs? she wondered. *If she did, would they know that I shouldn't be here? Could I explain it?*

Her continuous weakening left her doubtful about her ability to handle unknown situations. All she could do was marshal her strength for whatever it was she would face to secure additional power to hunt down Victor Daniels.

And I cannot waste that on some miserable cabbie.

With dusk settling in, Leanne made her way to the back of the house, exited it, and then walked out of the backyard. She wore shapeless clothing and leaned on the dull, battered steel cane she had found in the woman's home.

When she reached the street, Leanne paused and tilted her head up slightly. She closed her eyes and let the noise of the surroundings wash over her. Her nostrils flared, and she reached out with every sense, seeking the slim trail that she knew was there.

And she caught a hint of it, a whiff of power twisting through the air.

Leanne opened her eyes, smiling for the first time in days. She continued along the street, with the cemetery on her left-hand side. As she passed the wide opening into the burial ground, Leanne saw the name, *Edgewood Cemetery*, on a bronze sign secured to the right post.

Edgewood, she thought, glancing at the houses around the cemetery. *Not many woods left here.*

Leanne limped past the long, wrought-iron fence and the well-kept homes, focusing her thoughts on the power in the air. It grew stronger with every step, and her pace increased, a deep hunger driving her forward.

If all went well, Leanne would have regained her strength and feasted on fresh meat before the night was through.

CHAPTER 35:
A FLASH FLOOD

Justin and Jared Sandock hurried along the narrow game trail that cut through the woods along the edge of the Sunny Fields Golf Course. Raindrops crashed into the leaves above them, and when the wind shifted, the rain was driven sideways into the teens' exposed skin. Justin felt miserable, and a glance at his brother showed Jared was suffering as well.

Mario, their boss at the golf course, had kept them late, scrubbing the toilets in the women's room. And all because the brothers had tried to skip the last two stalls.

Mario, unfortunately, had done three years in the navy, and he knew what to look for when people were trying to skip out on doing their job.

Justin's hands ached from the work, which he had been forced to do twice since Mario made them clean the entire restroom again.

We only wanted to get home before the rain, Justin thought. He knew it wasn't true though. Neither one of them liked cleaning the bathrooms. Mowing the lawns and watering the flowers was what they had been hired to do.

None of this janitor stuff, Justin thought bitterly. If he had known that when he was hired, Justin wouldn't have taken the job.

"This is terrible," Jared complained.

"I know," Justin answered, trying to ignore the rain. "We're almost home."

"This is stupid," Jared added.

Justin rolled his eyes and focused on the trail. Mud splashed up around his white sneakers, and he let out a groan of disgust. He would have to clean them before his next shift. Not only was the golf course particular about the dress code, but Mario made sure everyone followed it.

The trail dipped down and curved slightly, bringing them to a small stream. With the heavy and sudden rain, the water moved faster than usual. Yet Justin knew he and his brother could cross it easily. Both boys ran the hurdles for the high school track team, and a three-foot-wide stream wasn't anything for them to be concerned with.

Justin broke into a jog and sprang from one side to the other, clearing the water easily. He moved further up the trail to give his brother room. After traveling another eight or nine feet up, Justin turned around to ask Jared a question, but his brother wasn't there.

Confused, he backtracked to the stream and stopped, horrified and shocked.

Jared lay face down in the water, another boy straddling over him and keeping Jared's head submerged.

It wasn't the fact that someone was drowning his brother that had frozen Justin in place.

It was the terrible realization that the water was passing through the killer as if he weren't there.

Fear drowned him in panic and a strangled scream escaped Justin's throat as he turned and fled.

Branches slapped at his face and roots pulled at his feet. First, one sneaker was torn off, then another, and Justin ran along the trail in his socks. He let out a pained scream as a sharp object stabbed the bottom of his left foot, and he spun and twisted, crashing into a tree. The stump of a branch pierced the side of his throat, and he hung there for a moment.

Then he saw the strange boy who had drowned his brother appear on the path, and Justin pushed himself off the tree. The jagged end of the branch jerked out of his neck, and he managed four steps before he pitched forward and crashed onto the trail.

He felt weak and lightheaded as he dug his fingers into the muddy ground and tried to pull himself forward, to get away from the achingly cold sensation creeping up on him.

Justin's vision narrowed, shrank, and then left him blind as he sank to the earth. He struggled for breath, yet his lungs refused to work. His heartbeat became erratic, and then it stopped.

"You can't go yet," a voice whispered. "Your brother wants company."

A cold hand wrapped around Justin's arm and in the stillness of his mind, Justin screamed.

Chapter 36

Too Much Time in the Air

Victor and Tom had unpacked, and the boy was in one of the hotel room's beds, fast asleep.

A forceful knock sounded at the door and, with a sigh, Victor stood up and went to it. He didn't bother looking through the peephole before he unlocked the door and opened it.

"Hello," Sara said, stepping into the room, her voice loud and boisterous. She grinned at Victor as she passed him, then the smile faltered, and a look of embarrassment fell over her face. "Oh, I'm sorry. I didn't realize you had your son with you."

Tom snored and rolled over. His left arm, with its vivid, pink scar on the stump of his upper arm, fell out of the blanket.

"He could sleep through the end of the world when he's tired," Victor said, giving the detective a reassuring smile. He adjusted the blanket on Tom, then went to the air conditioner's controls and turned it down another degree.

"Take a seat, Sara," Victor said, motioning towards the chairs near the curtained windows. When they were both seated, he asked, "How did it go?"

"Very well, thank you," Sara said. "We got a full confession, had him arraigned, and now he's waiting in a cell. I'm sure his lawyer will try to have the confession retracted, but the State's attorney will have to battle that out."

"I'm glad to hear it," Victor said.

"What about you?" Sara asked, leaning closer. "You look worn out. Have you been chasing this ghost without me?"

Victor shook his head, considered informing the detective about

Stefan Korzh, but then decided to keep the information to himself. "No. Just worn out from parenting."

"Ah," she said and settled back into the chair. "Have you checked the news or anything?"

"No," he replied. "I haven't been looking at it."

"There have been four more deaths," Sara said. "People are being evacuated out of the area, and the state and federal government are sending in teams to test the air quality, water, and soil."

"Four more drownings," Victor murmured.

Sara shook her head. "Deaths. Three were drownings. One was deemed accidental."

"Then how is it linked to the others?" Victor asked, confused.

"His brother was found face down in a stream," she explained, "and all the evidence points to the accidental death occurring as a result of the boy running from something."

"This needs to stop," Victor said, anger rising within him. He stood up and paced the room, glancing at Tom to make certain he didn't wake the boy.

"I agree," Sara said. "The question is, what do we do when we find the object? Do we destroy it? Do we imprison it?"

"We'll have to hold it," Victor said, returning to his seat. "I'll reach out to my friend again, see if he's found any information. Other than that, I believe I'm all set for supplies. And I should have enough rounds."

"I think we should split up the search," Sara said after a moment of silence.

Victor looked at her, surprised. "That's not the best idea."

"I know," she agreed. "But the situation calls for it. Whoever this ghost is, he's getting stronger with each death. At least that's what it feels like to me. Or else he's getting more confident, what with multiple murders in a single day. So, while we're putting ourselves at a disadvantage in regards to safety, I think we have to. Too many people are dying."

Victor gave a short, bitter nod. He knew she was right.

"I'm not going to try and do anything heroic," Sara added. "All I want is to find where the object is, then we can tackle it together."

"I've got an extra shotgun in the car," Victor said. "And I'm sure Tom packed a few items that will help as well."

She shot him a concerned glance. "What?"

"Tom," Victor said. "I'm sure he brought stuff as well. Iron, salt. I know he grabbed the lead-lined bag, so we can secure whatever the item might be."

"No," Sara said, shaking her head. "Not that. That I understood. My question is, is Tom going out?"

"Why wouldn't I be?" Tom asked.

The boy pushed himself up into a sitting position, rubbing at his eyes. He stifled a yawn, then continued. "I've hunted them before."

"You can't be serious," Sara said.

He waggled the stump of his arm at her, a grim expression on his face. "I am. Pick up my prosthetic."

Sara raised an eyebrow, but she did as Tom said. She turned the false limb over in her hands and said, "It's heavy. Wait, is this iron inlay?"

"Yes," Tom said.

"He had it done so he could defend himself," Victor said.

"What are you talking about?" Sara asked. "I am thoroughly confused."

"Sit back, detective," Victor said. "I'm going to tell you about myself and Tom, and how we got here."

Victor waited until she laid the prosthetic back on the dresser and then he told her about Erin, Tom's parents, and Stefan Korzh.

It was not a pleasant tale.

CHAPTER 37

AT THE SAFE HOUSE

The home was small, nothing more than a bungalow tucked away in the middle of suburban Philadelphia.

Stefan waited until two in the morning before he pulled into the driveway and parked the car in the garage. His body shook from a mixture of muscle fatigue and caffeine tablets he had been chewing since leaving the vicinity of Fox Cat Hollow. When he let himself into the house, Stefan quickly punched in the security code and limped to the sink. He let the cold water run, leaned over and ducked his head under it.

The water was a balm against his skin, and he stripped off the eye-patch, massaging the tender skin around it. Finally, Stefan took a drink from the running tap, then turned it off and left the kitchen. Motion sensors responded to him, and the lights came on. A fine layer of dust coated everything, which Stefan ignored as he dropped tiredly into a chair.

He closed his eye and tried to wrap his thoughts around the situation.

For a long period, he did nothing, merely letting ideas and images move at their own pace.

Soon, a solid picture of the situation he was in presented itself.

My father, Stefan thought, *has betrayed me. No big surprise there. The only surprising factor is Victor Daniels.*

The memory of the man caused Stefan to frown.

Daniels was an amateur, a hack at best. And yet the man had gotten the drop on Stefan. If Daniels hadn't been trying to save his son, Stefan had no doubt he would be trapped in whatever item his father had prepared for him.

The thought of his father brought Stefan thinking back to his family, and to the arrival of his half-sister. He grimaced at the prospect of Ariana and Daniels working in conjunction.

And that boy, Stefan thought, opening his eye and staring at the ceiling. *That boy is a strong one. He'll give me a run for my money.*

A smile crossed Stefan's face, and he shook his head.

He had a grudging admiration for the boy. Amateur or not, Tom Daniels had been fully prepared to blow up the warehouse.

He did blow up the warehouse, Stefan thought bitterly, remembering the blast. Then he stiffened and straightened up.

I didn't secure the hard drives, he realized. *Everything's on them. What if they took the drives?*

He shook his head, refusing to believe they would have had any interest in the equipment.

All Daniels wanted was his son, Stefan thought. Then he hesitated and asked himself, *but what about Ariana?*

A knock at the door launched him out of his chair and caused his heart to quicken.

The knock was repeated, and a stern voice declared, "This is the Burlington Police."

Fuming, Stefan walked to the door, forced a bland smile onto his face, and opened it.

A tall police officer stood on the doorstep. The man was in his early twenties and taller than Stefan. Stefan watched as the officer glanced around the room, and his anger increased. The officer's chin and the set of his eyes resembled those of Ivan Denisovich.

A glance at the officer's name badge stated that the man was Officer I. Colette, 3 Yrs. Service as a member of the Burlington PD.

Stefan forced his heart to slow, his smile to widen.

Colette was the name of a family that specialized in antiques.

And his father had made many trips to Philadelphia.

Many, Stefan thought.

"May I help you, officer?" Stefan asked.

"We had a complaint that someone had broken in," the man responded. "Do you have any proof of residency?"

"I do," Stefan said, and a furtive look at the officer's body-camera showed the red light, which would indicate if it was recording, wasn't lit. Stefan smiled. "I do. I have my wallet and my contract in the drawer of the hall table behind me. If I may?"

The officer nodded, and Stefan was pleased to see that the man's SUV was pulled up in such a way that the dash-cam wouldn't record anything.

As Stefan turned away and walked to the table, he heard the police dispatcher call in, and the officer replied, "Roger, Two Alpha Five on site."

Two Alpha Five, Stefan thought, opening the drawer. Within it was a small, .22 caliber semi-automatic with a suppressor. Stefan pulled the weapon free with an easy motion, turned and put a single round through the throat of the officer. The bullet tore into the left side of the man's neck, and Stefan was impressed with how quickly the officer slapped a hand over the wound.

But his struggle to live meant he couldn't draw his weapon, which was what Stefan had planned on. Two strides brought him back to the door, and as the officer reached out with his left hand, Stefan shot him twice in the right knee, dropping the man to the floor.

Reaching down, Stefan grabbed the man by the back of his shirt and dragged him into the house, and he kicked the door closed. He stripped the man's radio off, and as Officer Colette struggled to get up, Stefan shot him through the left thigh.

Squatting down beside the dying man, Stefan poked him in the forehead with the end of the suppressor. Rage and fear warred in the man's eyes, and Stefan was curious as to which would win out in the end.

"I bet your name's Ivan, isn't it," Stefan said conversationally.

A slight widening of Officer Colette's eyes told him it was.

"You don't have much time here, Officer Ivan Colette," Stefan continued, "so, I'll cut to the chase. I'm fairly certain we're brothers."

The officer's eyes fixed on him, and Stefan realized their eyes were identical.

"Yes, you see it too," Stefan said softly. "Seems like Dad got around far more than I ever suspected. As you can tell, I'm not a fan of the family. But brothers, well, we should certainly look like brothers, right?"

Stefan lifted the pistol, put the barrel at an angle against the man's left eye, and pulled the trigger. As the eye was vaporized, the bullet thudded into the far wall.

I can't forget to dig that one out, he thought as the officer writhed on the floor.

Stefan stood up, stepped back, and looked down at the man.

"I hate you," Stefan said. "I hate you all."

And he emptied the pistol into the man's groin.

***

Stefan knew the police weren't stupid. The prisons and jails had a healthy population of individuals who had made that mistake, and Stefan refused to be a member of that group.

His rage had cost him any sort of rest.

Once the officer had died, Stefan had been forced to butcher the man in a quick and messy fashion. With the body's remains secured in a pair of large canvas bags and wearing Officer Colette's oversized clothing along with a backpack, Stefan loaded up the remnants into the cruiser. Humming to himself, Stefan then drove it to an abandoned building only a few streets away. He pried out the radio, took the man's cellphone, and located the vehicle's GPS system. Stefan took these with him as he left the vehicle and the body behind.

"Unit Alpha, respond," the dispatcher said.

It was a male voice, one Stefan didn't recognize from his earlier call-ins with the officer's radio.

"This is two Alpha five," Stefan said, pitching his voice low.

"Location?" the man asked.

Stefan rolled his eyes. *I'll never get it done if they keep harassing me.*

He glanced around and saw an all-night convenience store at the corner. Smiling, Stefan said into the radio, "Dispatch, two Alpha five is about to take another twenty, corner of Hutch and 5th Street."

The dispatcher sighed. "Again?"

Evidently the dispatchers are little gossips, Stefan thought, frowning. "Bad stomach. Going to try to make it to the end of the shift. Two Alpha five, out."

The dispatcher said something Stefan didn't catch, but it didn't matter.

He was almost done.

Three streets to the north and Stefan found the alley with the sewer grate he was looking for. The electronic devices went in, and off Stefan went to another alley, where he stripped the uniform off. From the backpack, he removed fresh clothes and sneakers and several bottles of lighter fluid. He spread the uniform out, doused it with fluid, and set it on fire. Stefan watched the flames briefly, then wiped down the bottles and tossed them into another sewer grate.

And now, he thought bitterly, *I have to go and clean the damned house.*

Stefan adjusted his eye patch, stuffed his hands in his pockets, and started the long walk home.

CHAPTER 38:
DEVOLVING INTO DESPAIR

The house was huge and had it been made of wood instead of brick, it would have been one of the finer homes in the antebellum South.

Leanne sat on an overturned trash barrel in a small shed that stank of chemicals and grass clippings. From her perch, she could see the back of 125 Berkley Street. Several ducks glided on the calm surface of a pond, leaving small trails behind them. Tall cats' tails grew along the edges and moved with the occasional breeze.

And at the edge of the water, sitting in a wooden chair and drinking from a tall glass, was the man she had to kill.

Power radiated from him, so strong she could almost see it with the naked eye.

She knew from the man's appearance that he would not be an easy individual to slay.

His bald head was scarred, and his left ear was badly mangled. He was missing fingers on one hand, and his posture, even sitting in the chair, told her that he was a man accustomed to violence.

But it wasn't the physicality of the man that concerned her, it was the sheer willpower that she could sense. The dominance of anything living or dead.

For the first time, Leanne was unsure of herself.

Never had she doubted her ability to take what she wanted, to defeat whomever she must, but the man in the chair made her do just that.

I have no choice, Leanne thought. *There is no other strong enough. Not even close. I must siphon his if I am to kill Victor Daniels.*

With a sigh, she settled in to wait.

***

Sweat dripped down Ariana's back as she dried her face with a towel. She had pushed herself beyond her limits, and her muscles already ached.

I'll feel this one in the morning, she thought ruefully as she walked into the kitchen. She took a Gatorade out of the refrigerator and opened it. Within a minute, she had emptied half of the bottle. She wiped her face again, then carried both the drink and the towel into her front room. Ariana opened the sliding door and stepped out onto her apartment's small balcony.

The sun had crested the horizon, and she could hear cars start up as people began their working day.

She smiled as she thought about a normal job. One where she went into an office or some sort of establishment and worked for eight and a half hours.

I don't have that discipline, she thought, taking a sip from her Gatorade. *I'd hit somebody in the first hour. And customer service? Nope, no way.*

Ariana finished her drink, put the cap back on and grinned.

I'll stick with killing people and hunting ghosts.

The grin faltered, then faded as she went back into her home. She closed the door, drew the curtain, and sat down on the couch.

Ghosts, she thought. *More specifically one ghost.*

Ivan Denisovich Korzh.

A blunt hammer of emotions slammed into her chest as she thought of her father and his betrayal.

His attempt to gather her unto his ghostly fold was understandable.

The murder of her mother was not.

I can't confront him about it, she thought. *He's too strong. It will have to be done subtly, and without any hint as to my knowledge of the killing. And when it's done, I'll find Anne Le Morte and destroy her, too.*

Ariana closed her eyes and fought back the desire to find the doll first, to learn where her mother's spirit was being kept.

To do so might alert Ivan Denisovich, and she had no desire to do that.

No, Ariana thought. *I don't want my father to know until the last moment what is happening and why.*

Her phone chimed and interrupted her train of thought. Frowning, she leaned over and picked it up.

It was a text from Victor.

Busy?

Always, she wrote. *What's up?*

Drownings in Pennsylvania. A lot.

Ariana wrote, *Sorry. I'm on my way out to a job.*

Then, before she hit send, she considered her situation.

Victor had shown his determination at Stefan's compound. And he could, if necessary, help her deal with her father.

She erased the message and wrote. *Where?*

He sent her the address of a hotel and Ariana went into her gear room.

As she surveyed the weapons, she thought about her half-brother.

He'll have to go before our father, Ariana thought. *I'll have to talk to Victor about that too.*

And she buried her feelings for the man beneath her mounting hatred.

CHAPTER 39

RESTLESS SLEEP

Monica Page lay on her back and stared up at the ceiling. Her eyes traced the cracks in the plaster, lingering for a moment on the husks of insects in the ceiling lamp's globe. She winced as the baby-monitor squawked into life.

Eliot's cry broke the stillness of the room, and Monica let out a ragged sigh.

She pushed herself up, and the blankets fell down around her waist. Eliot whimpered, then went silent. Monica looked at the monitor, hesitated, then took her pack of Parliaments off the bed-side table and shook out a cigarette. She used the disposable pink Bic lighter to light the cigarette, and she drew the calming smoke into her lungs. When she exhaled, Monica glanced at the monitor again and saw the red light flicker, but she didn't hear any noise.

Did he fall back asleep? she wondered, inhaling again. A vain hope formed in her chest, and she wondered if she might be able to sleep for another hour or two. Eliot had been up for most of the night with a fever and Monica had gotten precious little sleep.

I just want to finish this cigarette, she thought. *Then I'll lie down.*

She had given him Tylenol at one in the morning, and it wasn't due to wear off.

Eliot screamed.

It was a horrific sound that stabbed Monica in the pit of her stomach and launched her out of bed. Her half-smoked cigarette fell to the floor, and she ran out of the room, chest heaving by the time she reached Eliot's open door.

The two-year-old boy lay face up in his crib, an empty bottle of water beside him, and another figure stood in the crib over him.

Without hesitation, Monica snatched up the Winnie-the-Pooh lamp by the door and hurled it at the invader.

But the light passed through the stranger and shattered against the far wall.

Certain that her eyes had played a trick on her, Monica glanced around the room, searching for a weapon. She spotted a large, framed picture of the cover for *Goodnight Moon* and she ripped it off the wall.

Turning to face the stranger, who now stood beside the crib, Monica was surprised to see it was a child, a boy of perhaps 10.

That fact did not stop her from lunging forward and swinging the picture at his head.

The frame passed through the boy, and the force of the intended blow twisted her around, caused her to lose her balance, and sent her down to one knee.

An impossibly cold wave of air wrapped around her and the boy leaned close.

"The child's mother was on the ship, too," the boy said in a distant voice.

Monica screamed as the stranger grabbed her by the hair and without another word dragged her out of the room. She stopped screaming and clawed at the walls and carpet, trying to seek some sort of handhold, some way to stop herself.

The child was incredibly strong, and each time she managed a grip, he gave a tug, and she howled as another fingernail was torn out of her and left in the wall.

Monica didn't try to speak to the murderer, she was furious. Eliot, she knew, was dead.

And the boy dragging her down the hall, the cold, incorporeal child, had done it.

They reached the bathroom, and the boy threw her casually against the tub. The impact dislocated her shoulder and caused Monica to black out for a moment.

When her head cleared, she saw the door was open as the boy squatted down in front of the pedestal sink, examining the pipes.

Instead of trying to escape, Monica reached up, grabbed hold of the shower curtain and liner, and pulled them down with one hand.

With a shriek of rage, she launched herself at the boy, intent on smothering him.

But she passed through him, the child's body so cold that she let out a scream of pain. She landed on her dislocated shoulder, vomited from the pain, and rolled on her back in time to see the stranger rip the flex-pipe out of the sink. Hot water splashed across her as the boy turned to face her.

"My mother fought for me, too," he said. "I suppose all mothers do."

With his free hand, he grabbed her by the face and then shoved the flex-pipe into her mouth. He smiled as he held her mouth closed around the hot material. Painfully hot water coursed down her throat and she understood that in a few seconds she would need to breathe, and it would be the water that filled her lungs.

"Did you sing to him?" the stranger asked. "I'm sure you did. My mother did."

Monica struggled against the boy, but it was no use, she couldn't free herself.

"My mother always did," he whispered, and then he smiled and watched as Monica tried to take a breath through her nose.

"No," he said, adjusting his grip to pinch her nose closed, "that's not fair."

And with that simple act, he forced her to inhale the water and start the long, slow process of drowning.

CHAPTER 40

PLANS AND PREPARATIONS

The phone rang, and Victor answered it when he saw Shane Ryan's name.

"Victor," Shane said cheerfully. "How are you holding up?"

"I'll make it," Victor answered.

Shane laughed and said, "Glad to hear it. So, listen, I reached out to some people and finally got a straight answer from someone who knows their stuff. You need to get a hold of the item, and you need to secure it, which I'm pretty sure you were planning on anyway."

"Yes," Victor agreed. "That's step one."

"Figured," Shane said. "Now, step two is where it becomes iffy, and sometimes, well, it doesn't always go as planned."

"How so?" Victor asked.

"It really depends on how many spirits are bound to the ghost in the item." Shane hesitated and then continued. "So, let's say your ghost has ten people that it's bound to. When you destroy the item, you're going to free them, but the blast radius from the destruction of the object increases with each spirit. Do you see what I'm getting at?"

"I think so," Victor said. "Is there a basic formula?"

"I wish," Shane said. "My friend said that you could expect a hundred-foot radius for every couple of spirits. Plus, if the ghost who imprisoned them is really powerful, those parameters are going to magnify. Basically, if you think this entity is strong, you figure out a way to destroy the item where no one else is around. And I mean no one. You might have to drive the damned thing out to Ohio or someplace else that's flat and open."

"Damn," Victor said, sighing. "Thank you."

Tom came out of the bathroom and sat down with his prosthetic. Victor gave a short wave to the teen, and the boy smiled and waved back.

"Sure," Shane said. "Just a quick question, how many people are trapped now?"

Victor thought about it, then said, "Fourteen at last count. Probably more by now."

"Okay," Shane said. "When you get your hands on it, and you're ready to destroy it, let me know. I might be able to help."

"Alright. Thank you again," Victor said, and he ended the call.

Looking over at Tom, he asked, "How are you doing?"

Tom looked up from adjusting the prosthetic and said, "Okay. I was going to take a walk."

Victor almost asked Tom if he had his iron with him, but he smiled, remembering the inlay and nodded. "Sounds good. Be back in an hour or so, alright?"

"Sure," Tom said, and he left the room, holding the door open for Sara. The detective greeted the teen and then closed the door behind him.

Her eyes were dark with lack of sleep, and she yawned as she leaned against the wall.

"Where's he off to?" she asked.

"A walk," Victor answered.

"I might do the same in a bit," Sara said, "see if I can wake up."

Victor nodded, and the two of them sat down as the morning sunlight streamed in through the open slider. "I requested some help."

"From your friend?" Sara asked. "The one who might know about the spirits bound to others?"

Victor shook his head. "No. Although, I did hear back from him. He told me that if we destroy the item, then the others will be released. Unfortunately, we'll need to make certain we do that in an open area."

Sara frowned, and Victor added, "When the item is destroyed, there will be an explosion. A release of energy. The stronger the ghost, and the more spirits attached to it, the bigger the explosion will be."

"How big?" Sara asked.

"My friend suggested that we find an open space in one of the Midwest states," Victor answered.

"Wow," Sara said. Then she shook her head and asked, "Alright, if you weren't talking about him, then who were you talking about?"

Victor hesitated before he answered, "She introduced herself as Betty."

Sara was silent for a moment. Finally, she said, "Can she help?"

"That is a definite *yes*," Victor said. "I could explain how, but it would take too long. The woman is exceptionally skilled."

"She is an exceptional pain," Sara retorted. "But I've worked with difficult people before, and the whole point is to get this ghost secured, and the others released."

"My thoughts exactly," Victor said.

"When is Tom coming back?" Sara asked.

"Within an hour," Victor replied. "I'd like to use that time to map out the deaths that we know of and get our equipment ready."

"Sounds like a good idea to me," Sara said.

"I picked this up this morning from the lobby," Victor said, picking up a foldout street map of the area. He spread it out on the small table and picked up a red pen. "I also spent a good chunk of time finding out where the different people died."

Using a notepad, Victor began to mark the different streets and house numbers where people had been killed. In addition to that, he placed a number beside each death with Nancy as victim one.

"These are the fourteen that we know about," Victor said, "and all the deaths radiate from Nancy's house."

"Which means the item is either in her place or nearby," Sara said.

Victor nodded. "We can start with her house and do a more thorough search."

"I'll take her house," Sara said, "you and Tom can take her next-door neighbor's."

"I'd like to wait for Betty," he said, almost saying Ariana instead.

"We don't have time, Victor," Sara said. "I'm not saying let's get this done, so I don't have to deal with her. I'm saying let's get this done, so no one else dies."

"Yeah," Victor said, "you're right."

"I'll grab my gear and bring it back," Sara said, standing up. "As soon as Tom's here, we'll take a ride out to Nancy's place and start the search."

"Okay," Victor said and picked up his phone as Sara left the room. He sent Ariana a text to let her know the change of plans and then went to his suitcase. Victor unlocked it, moved his clothes, and removed his shotgun.

The cold steel felt good in his hands, and with a growing sense of anticipation, he carried the weapon to the table and waited for Sara to return.

CHAPTER 41

AN INTERVIEW

Tom kept to the left side of the road as he walked, birdsong and squirrel chatter loud in the trees. He reached a small bridge, paused, then turned off the road to follow a weathered path down to the banks of a small and sluggish stream. The banks were surprisingly free of litter, and there were only a few random lines of graffiti on the concrete pylons and bridge supports.

Tom sat down in the dew-damp grass and picked up a handful of small stones. He tossed them one at a time into the water, enjoying the way the ripples vanished as the stones sank.

When he reached down for another handful, he felt a cold breeze caress his back and gooseflesh appeared on his arm.

With a shiver, Tom straightened up and glanced around. He looked back to the stream and stopped.

A boy stood a few feet in front of him. Tom had no doubt it was the ghost they had been searching for.

The child's clothes were outdated by a century or more, and while he was almost fully formed, there were parts of the boy's body where Tom could see hints of the water through him.

"Hello," Tom said, keeping his nervousness in check.

"Hello," the boy answered. He squinted and asked, "What's wrong with your left arm?"

Tom raised the arm and showed the dead boy the prosthetic. "It's a false arm."

"How did you lose it?" The child's question was one of polite interest, with nothing sinister behind it.

"An accident," Tom answered vaguely. "My name's Tom, what's

yours?"

The boy ignored the question. A frown settled over his face, and he stated, "There were no one-armed people on the ship. Not a one. You won't do any good."

The ghost began to fade, and Tom asked, "What ship?"

For a second the dead boy lingered, half-formed, then he became solid again.

"The ship that sank," the boy replied. "We were there, hundreds of us. We tried to get off the ship, but it went down too quickly. But everything will be better soon."

"Oh yeah?" Tom asked, and he tried to think of a way to question the dead boy about what he might be bound to.

"Yes," the child beamed. "As soon as I have all of the passengers, then we'll finish the trip."

"Really?" Tom struggled and then blurted out, "Why?"

"Because I want to," the boy stated. An angry look flashed across the child's face. "I wanted the trip. I liked it. I had my ticket. But I'm going to finish my trip, just as soon as everyone's on board."

The dead child vanished, leaving Tom on the bank with a thundering heart.

Could it be a ticket? Tom thought, getting to his feet. *Was the trip that important to him?*

He hesitated, unsure as to whether or not the information was significant.

I need to tell Victor, Tom decided, turning around and following the path back up the road. *He'll know what to do.*

He always does.

Chapter 42

Hunting the Dead

"A ticket?" Sara asked.

Tom nodded, and Victor powered up his laptop. Sitting down in front of it, Victor selected images and typed in the name of the ship and the word 'ticket' into the search engine.

The results came up a moment later.

"This," Victor said, turning the screen to face Tom and Sara, "is what we're looking for."

"All this death," Sara murmured, leaning closer, "attached to such a small thing."

"Yes," Victor said. "Are you ready?"

"Who can ever say they're ready for something like this?" Sara asked. "Want me to drive?"

"Please," Victor answered.

They packed up their equipment, and Victor made certain to tuck away his lock picking tools. He doubted he would find the house unlocked.

"Tom," Victor said, and the teen looked over at him. "Come here."

Tom walked over, and Victor embraced him, the boy giving him a strong hug back. He gave the boy a quick kiss on the top of his head, "You are my son, and I love you."

Tom nodded, wiped his eyes, and said in a husky voice, "I love you, too."

Detective Sara Milton opened the door, and the three of them left. They moved quickly down the hall and took the stairs to the first floor. The ride in Sara's rental car was short, and when they arrived at Nancy's house, the street had an odd sense of desertion to it. Some of the doors on the houses were sealed off with red tape, and at his questioning glance, Sara answered, "Quarantine. They're not sure what's going on, so they've sealed the buildings. Let's hope they haven't put any sensors in."

"Would they do that?" Tom asked, surprised.

Sara shrugged as she shut off the car and they got out. "They might. I don't know how serious the federal government is taking the matter. My new friend on the police here doesn't know. Seems like they've been cut out of the loop."

"Only one way to find out," Victor said.

Sara nodded. "I'll take Nancy's house as we agreed. You two search her neighbor's, I think his name was Gilbert, and we'll go from there."

"Okay," Victor said. "Good luck."

"Same," Sara said, and they split up.

Tom walked close to Victor as they crossed the sidewalk and went around to the door that led into the man's garage. It was locked, and in far better shape than Nancy's had been.

"Do you want to try this one?" Tom asked.

"No," Victor said, shaking his head. "The police are supposed to have stepped up patrols. We'll try the back door."

With that said, the two of them walked around the back together, and Victor led the way up the stairs to the porch. He pulled out his lock pick set and had the door open in a few minutes.

"Wow," Tom said, "you would have made a good thief."

Victor felt his face flush with a mixture of pride and embarrassment as he put his tools away. He took out his shotgun and looked over at Tom. An expression that was part anticipation and fear overtook the boy's face, and had Victor feel afraid for him.

As skilled as Tom was, he was still a boy.

But Victor didn't falter. Instead, he asked, "Do you have what you need?"

Tom lifted his prosthetic, and in the false hand, he held the lead-lined bag. On his right hand was an iron ring, and Victor knew they were as ready as could be.

Feeling as though he was about to step into a pool of murky water, Victor entered the dark house.

***

Sara Milton shivered as she crossed the threshold of the front door into Nancy's house. The temperature was colder than the previous time she and Victor had been in the building.

She paused to zip up the hooded sweatshirt she had worn, and to tug on the white cotton gloves Victor had given her. In her left hand, she held a Zip-lock freezer bag filled with salt. If she found the boarding pass, she'd need to stuff it in and hope the salt contained the ghost.

I don't need to run outside with it, she thought. *I have to secure it and set it down. Then we can transfer it to Victor's bag.*

She had no doubt that the ticket would be in Nancy's house. All the evidence pointed to it being in that location. Nancy had been the first death. The dead had gathered in the woman's home. It was a simple and logical process. Which was why she had sent Victor and Tom into the neighbor's house.

Sara couldn't bear the thought of having Tom's death on her conscience.

Victor's would be bad enough, she thought, heading for the stairs. *But the boy, that would be too much.*

After a moment of hesitation, Sara placed the heavy bag in one of the sweatshirt's pockets. She would need both hands for the shotgun Victor had insisted on. Sara remembered her first encounter with a ghost, and with King Kincaid carrying a shotgun loaded with rock-salt. The old man had been a skilled shot, and he had proven that the weapon could be used successfully for offense or defense.

But Sara preferred offense.

Aggression suited her best.

Holding the gun easily, she climbed the stairs. Her teeth chattered with every step, and her breath billowed out of her mouth in great white clouds. When she reached the hallway, she stopped and looked in surprise.

All she could see were the dead.

Each one turned to face her, their eyes dull and confused.

And there were far more than fourteen.

CHAPTER 43

POOR DECISION-MAKING SKILLS

Leanne limped along the edge of the road and then cut across the unkempt lawn of the large brick house. The sun had risen only a short time before, and her body was in pain from the uncomfortable position she had remained in while sleeping in the shed.

But the reward would be well worth the aggravation.

She had watched the house for most of the night, and the owner had gone to sleep well after midnight. He had been drinking the entire time.

Leanne had no doubt that the man would be dead drunk in his bed, and there was no one else in the home with him. Of that, she was certain.

Several times she had thought he had company, but Leanne hadn't been able to see anyone. Even when he was on his porch and having a conversation with some unseen person.

Someone I should see, Leanne thought bitterly. There was a sense about the property, as if the dead lurked about the building and the landscape. The fact that she could not see them stung bitterly, and her mouth twisted into a grimace.

The man had continued drinking.

He's a fool, she thought, creeping toward the basement door. *Albeit a powerful one. Perhaps he might even sense the presence of the dead. Regardless, it will be a mercy to kill him.*

His drinking had left her feeling disgruntled, as had his chain-smoking.

The man's flesh would be far too foul to eat.

Focus now, she thought. *I may have to use some of my strength to force the door.*

Leanne cleared her mind as she reached out and touched the doorknob. She twisted it once and nearly gasped in surprise.

The knob turned, and the door swung in on silent hinges.

She suppressed a joyous laugh and eased into the basement. Closing the door gently behind her, Leanne allowed her eyes to adjust to the dim light.

The basement was surprisingly devoid of clutter, consisting mainly of a washer, dryer, water heater, and a furnace that looked as though it might once have powered a steam engine. Pipes and wires crisscrossed the wide beams of the ceiling, and a set of stairs led up to the main floor.

Leanne limped toward it, pausing every few steps to listen.

Not a single sound reached her ears.

Smiling, she climbed the stairs, paused at the closed door at the top and then eased it open inch by inch. Soon, she found herself standing in a large kitchen, one that smelled of cigarettes, alcohol, and coffee. A single plate, knife, and fork stood in the drying rack at the sink, and they confirmed Leanne's belief that the man was alone in his home.

Now, she thought, glancing up at the tin ceiling, *where are you sleeping in this great big house of yours?*

She tried to smell him, but there was nothing to smell. Not a trace of sweat, or any peculiar odor. The stench of cigarettes was heavy, but it permeated everything and offered nothing by way of a trail.

Frowning, Leanne set off towards the center of the home.

She had made it a short distance from the kitchen when the door to that room slammed shut and locked itself. Above her came the creak of floorboards and Leanne looked around for a place to hide. An open doorway, a few feet to the right, caught her eye, and she limped toward it, slipping over the threshold before the owner of the house came to a stop somewhere on the upper floor.

Leanne found the doorknob and eased the door closed, leaving it open an inch so she might peer out and keep watch.

After several seconds, she heard him start to walk again. He descended a flight of stairs, the sound of his steps drawing closer. She gathered the last of her strength and prepared to throw open the door and launch herself at the man after he had passed by.

The footsteps reached the door and continued down the hall, and there was no one to see.

Not a soul.

Leanne almost let out a laugh, and she stepped back from the door.

A ghost, she thought. *And why shouldn't there be a ghost in a house this large?*

The door closed itself, and a male voice that spoke English with a thick German accent said, "You, Madam, should not be here."

A ghost, Leanne thought. *Nothing more.*

"Open the door," she commanded in a low voice. "I've no business with your kind this morning."

"Whether you have business with me or not is not yours to decide," the unseen ghost said from her left. "This is the home of my friend, and you are not welcome here."

Leanne ignored the dead man and approached the door, intent on letting herself out.

A cold hand took hold of her arm and stopped her, and no matter how she tried to twist herself free from his grasp, Leanne could not. She considered using her strength to escape, then rejected the idea.

No, she thought, taking a step backward. The ghost released her arm, and Leanne found a chair to sit in. *This can work to my advantage. He will bring his living friend to me soon enough, and then I will be able to escape this place. I will not squander the little strength that remains.*

"What is your name?" the ghost inquired.

"Leanne Le Monde," she replied. "And yours?"

"Carl," he answered. "I shall speak with my friend and tell him that you are here."

Yes, Leanne thought, closing her eyes and gathering her strength. *Tell him I am here. I want to see Victor Daniels sooner rather than later.*

***

Stefan sat on the back step of his safe house and rubbed tiredly at the muscles around his empty eye socket. He had slept fitfully after scouring the house of all evidence of the policeman he had murdered. In his hand, he held the .22 round that had passed through the man's eye and into the wall.

The police had yet to follow up with him, but Stefan knew it was only a matter of time. Law enforcement was predictable and effective because of it. Given time, they would realize that Stefan was responsible, or at least knew something about Officer Colette's disappearance. Stefan would need to wait until they reached out to him. Leaving before that would make him look guilty.

Anything will make me look guilty, he thought, pocketing the mashed bullet into his pocket. *It'll be a fine line to walk, but I've done it before, and I can do it again.*

He tried not to make killing police a habit. All it would take was one rogue police officer to decide Stefan was guilty, and then Stefan would wind up dead, the victim of a suspicious carjacking.

He grinned at the thought, stood up and went back into the house. In the living room, where he had murdered Officer Colette, several candles burned on the mantle. The cloying scent of honeysuckle filled the air, and the flames were reflected in the glass of a picture. Behind the glass was a black and white image of an old woman with glasses and a kindly face.

The scented candles hid the stench of cleaning chemicals and the photo, purchased in New York years earlier, would be passed off as one of his grandmother's.

Who died ten years ago today, officer, Stefan thought, practicing his lie. Each morning he would light the candles, and each morning he would prepare to tell that lie until either the smell of the chemicals was gone, or he had left town.

I can't leave town, he thought. *Not yet. I need to find out where Daniels is living and pay him and his brat back for ruining everything. Everything!*

And after them, he thought, regaining his composure. *Well, I'll take care of Ariana and Ivan Denisovich.*

Someone knocked on his door, and Stefan smiled. He glanced at the unknown woman on the mantle, feigned a grimace of sorrow, and opened the door.

A pair of Burlington police officers stood on the step, and Stefan asked in a soft voice, "May I help you?"

CHAPTER 44:
THE GANG'S ALL HERE

Sara felt as though she was wading through snow as she walked down the narrow hallway of Nancy's second floor. The dead looked at her, some with understanding and others without. An older man, looking as though he had been ready to go to bed when he was murdered, shook his head and hissed, "You need to get out, young lady!"

"Why?" Sara asked, coming to a stop.

"He's here," the dead man replied, "and he'll take you too!"

For the first time, Sara felt fear overwhelm her. It struck her in the pit of her stomach with the force of a fist, and she understood the real danger she was in. And how foolish she had been to not want to search in groups.

I'm not in a group, she thought, nodding and turning away from the dead man, *I'm alone.*

Sara stepped toward the stairs and froze.

A young boy stood before her, his form frightfully more solid than those of the others. The ghosts around him shrank away, some openly weeping at the sight of the boy.

"Hello," the dead child said, taking a step closer toward her.

Sara brought the shotgun up, but before her finger could squeeze the trigger, the boy flickered and was in front of her. His small hand touched hers, and she screamed in both shock and pain as the cold pierced the cotton gloves. Her fingers went numb and she dropped the weapon.

"Have you come for the trip?" he asked.

"No," Sara said, straightening up.

"That's a shame," the boy said, frowning. Then he smiled. "But you'll come anyway. I need another woman, and besides, everyone else is coming. It will be a wonderful time."

Sara tried to back away from him, her mind scrambling, seeking a path out of the house that didn't require passing him.

A window, she thought. *Better a broken leg than being dead.*

The dead boy smirked, and two of the doors in the hall slammed closed.

As the third swung on its hinges, Sara dove for it and found herself rolling across the floor of Nancy's bedroom.

The first sight to greet her eyes as she stood up was the master bathroom.

And as she watched, the faucet in the sink turned on, and water exploded into the basin.

She spun, eyes fixed on a window beside the bed, and she ran for it.

Yet the dead boy caught her by the back of her sweatshirt and she gasped as the breath was ripped out of her lungs. He jerked Sara off her feet and dragged her limp body towards the bathroom.

"I would tell you it isn't bad. Drowning," the boy said. "But that would be a lie, and I was told I shouldn't lie. So, I won't. Drowning is terrible. A heavy weight in your lungs. I can remember when I died. There were so many people in the water. Someone stepped on my head as I tried to swim up. I think they were trying to stand on me, which was silly. The water was too deep."

"Stop," Sara gasped, trying to free herself.

"No," the boy answered.

He dragged her into the bathroom, wrapped a hand in her short hair and leaned in close to whisper.

"I won't make you suffer," he said softly. "At least not that much."

And he shoved Sara's face into the bitterly cold water.

***

Ariana didn't recognize the car parked in front of the address Victor had given her.

She shrugged, got out of her own vehicle, and removed her shotgun. A glance up and down the street left her unsettled.

There was no movement.

Nothing.

Not even a mailman or someone out walking their dog. No wandering cats. Even the birds and the squirrels were silent.

Bad, Ariana thought. *This is bad. Worse than I thought it would be. What the hell has he gotten himself into?*

She took out a bandolier of extra shells and slipped it over her neck and shoulder. Finally, Ariana pulled on a pair of gloves laced with iron filings and flexed her fingers.

Right, she thought. *Let's get this done.*

Ariana crossed the sidewalk, strode up the walkway and let herself into the house.

"He's killing her!" a voice snapped, and Ariana jerked around, her finger tight on the shotgun's trigger.

The ghost of a tall old man stood in the shadow, his back straight and a look of command about him.

Ariana didn't ask him who.

"Where?" she demanded.

"Master bathroom," he replied, and Ariana raced up the stairs.

No other ghosts were visible, but from an open door, she heard running water.

She barreled through the doorway, the shotgun's stock tucked into her shoulder. As she turned the corner of the room, she saw the bathroom. The ghost of a young boy held a woman against the bathroom sink with one hand while he kept her head pressed down into the rising water with the other.

Ariana pulled the trigger.

***

Sara fell back, vomiting water and gasping for air. Her lungs screamed for oxygen and her back and arms burned with a rough pain.

She collapsed onto the bathroom floor and drew in great, shuddering breaths.

A stranger, armed with a shotgun and a bandolier of spare shells, approached her, squatting down beside Sara and grinning.

"Hey there," Betty said. "I'm betting this didn't work out the way you thought it would."

"No, Betty, it didn't," Sara said hoarsely.

"Call me, Ariana," the younger woman said. She glanced around and asked, "Where's Victor?"

"At the neighbor's house," Sara said, struggling into a sitting position.

The sound of a shotgun cut off Ariana's response.

CHAPTER 45:
VISITING THE NEIGHBOR

Victor reloaded the weapon, and he and Tom remained still. With his ears ringing from the blast of the shotgun in the close confines of the house, Victor's eyes darted around the room.

The two of them were in the kitchen, the far wall of which was now perforated by rock-salt.

Victor had seen a shape, a fast-moving ghost the size of a child and he didn't hesitate.

He pulled the trigger.

The enormity of their task suddenly made itself known.

We have to search this house and find one ticket, he thought. *A single item the size of a driver's license.*

How are we going to do that?

"Are you okay?" Tom asked in a low voice.

Victor nodded. "Really wishing we had a way to locate the boarding pass before this ghost kills us."

Tom gave a dry chuckle and nodded. "Yeah. That'd be nice."

The boy moved forward and quickly searched the cluttered countertop. Then he stopped and let out a laugh.

"What?" Victor asked, confused.

"Hot and cold," Tom answered, looking at him. "Like the game you play, when you're little. Something's hidden, and one person looks while somebody else gives clues."

"Hot you're close, cold you're not," Victor said, nodding.

"But in this case, cold means we're close," Tom said.

Victor jerked the shotgun back up and Tom dove to the floor. The ghost hurled itself across the room, and Victor shot it again. He hastily reloaded, not sure as to how long the ghost would take the second time.

"I'll take the lead," Tom said, getting back to his feet.

"No," Victor said, his eyes darting around the room.

"I have to." Tom's tone was serious. "I can feel it. *Him*, a lot better than you. You have to trust me."

Victor nodded, worried his voice would break with fear for the boy.

Tom closed his eyes, and Victor forced himself to remain calm.

"This way," Tom whispered, opening his eyes. He turned, and Victor followed. The air grew colder as they moved further into the house.

And despite the morning sun beyond the walls, the interior became darker.

Victor tightened his grip on the shotgun and waited for the ghost to appear.

***

Sara's lungs ached, and her stomach felt as though someone had stabbed a saw into it and twisted her guts around. She kept pace with Ariana, yet it was difficult. The woman moved quickly and confidently, and Sara understood that she was dealing with a professional. She remembered the irritation she had felt when she first met the young woman, and she was pleased that she hadn't tried to physically stop her.

Ariana's every move was as graceful as it was deadly. No motion was wasted, and nothing escaped her sight.

They exited the garage, heading towards Gilbert's house.

Instead of moving to the front, Ariana went around to the back. Sara almost asked why, but then she realized it would have been a stupid question.

Police, she thought. As mild as Victor Daniels was, he certainly wasn't a fool.

They turned the corner of the house, and Sara saw that the back door at the top of the porch was open. Halfway up the stairs, a shotgun sounded again, the windows of the house rattling in their frames.

Ariana ripped the door open and barreled into the home. A heartbeat later, as Sara followed her, the other woman's shotgun roared.

Sara crossed the threshold, and a voice screamed, "You're dead!"

Cold hands grabbed her around the waist and threw her. She hit an interior wall with enough force to knock pictures down, and the last sound she heard was another shotgun as she slipped into unconsciousness.

***

"Victor!"

He paused and glanced down the stairs. "Up here, Ariana!"

As his gaze swung back to Tom, Victor saw the teen lash out with his prosthetic and the dead boy who had materialized vanished.

"Where is it?" Victor asked. Three doors lead off from the hallway, and each was closed.

"The door at the far end," Tom answered. Ariana's footsteps pounded on the stairs.

"Look out!" she screamed, but it was too late.

A cold, hammer-like blow struck Victor in the small of the back and sent him to his knees. The force of the impact knocked the breath out of him and left him struggling, his chest heaving as Ariana fired her shotgun again.

He reached out, put his hand against the wall and tried to get to his feet, but his legs refused to support his weight.

In a moment, Ariana was at his side, helping him to his feet and supporting him, her face absent of any emotion. Her eyes danced with mad glee, a bloodlust that he hadn't seen in them before. With one hand, she leveled the shotgun at the ghost as the boy appeared again and pulled the trigger.

But the child was smarter than Victor had believed.

A second before the shotgun fired, the dead boy flickered out and then reappeared.

"No," the boy hissed, and he punched Ariana in the chest, sending her backward.

Victor fell with her, and then, as the ghost stood over them, Tom swung his arm.

The iron laced prosthetic passed through the dead boy, and the child screamed. Victor saw Tom shudder and stagger back.

"Get to the room," Victor said, his voice hoarse, "find the ticket."

"What about you?" Tom asked, and Victor heard the fear in his son's voice.

"We'll be fine," Victor said. His lower back ached, and his legs tingled. "Go."

Tom nodded, turned around and hurried down the hall. Victor watched Tom open the door and walk inside.

Ariana struggled into a sitting position, her face pale and drawn.

"Broken ribs," she said through clenched teeth. "At least two. Another hit like that and he might drive the damned things into my lungs."

"Where is he?" Victor asked, refusing to acknowledge the rising panic his legs were producing.

"He's a smart kid," Ariana answered. "He's learning. And I think he's figured out that we're not the threat."

The door at the end of the hall slammed shut, and the house shook.

"Oh no," Victor whispered, and he began to drag himself down the hall.

CHAPTER 46

ALONE, IN THE ROOM

Tom could feel the ticket as he stood in silence.

The room stank of old sweat and bad breath, of dirty clothes and half-forgotten meals.

It was the room of a bachelor who no longer cared about himself, and somewhere, hidden in the debris of a dead man's life, the boarding pass for the *Lady Elgin* waited.

The door slammed closed, and the room's temperature sank.

The boy appeared near the bed and looked at Tom warily. After a short time, the dead child said, "Hello. I am beginning to wonder."

"Wonder what?" Tom asked, trying to focus on the location of the pass.

"Whether I should bring you with me for the trip," the dead boy said. Tom watched the ghost walk to the bed and then sit down on it. "He was a pig."

"The man who lived here?" Tom asked.

The dead boy nodded.

"I didn't like him. I still don't like him," the child stated. "I am going make him stay under the water when we go out. What do you think about that?"

Tom shrugged. "I don't really have an opinion one way or the other."

The dead boy smiled. "Yes, you should come with me on the trip."

Tom hesitated, then asked, "Don't you want to move on? To go to heaven?"

"Of course, I do," the ghost said, his voice serious. "My mother's in heaven, and I want to be with her."

Tom started to speak, but the dead boy interrupted him.

"I want my trip first," the child snapped. "And I can't have it until everyone is onboard."

Silence filled the room, and in the hallway beyond, Tom heard someone moving towards the door.

The bed, Tom realized. *The boarding pass is under the bed.*

He tightened his grip on the lead-lined bag as the dead boy asked, "Do you think you can stop me?"

"Yes," Tom said, and he meant it.

"How?" the ghost asked. "You can send me away, for a moment or two, when you strike me. But I always come back."

"And what about the shotguns?" Tom asked, stepping towards the bed and keeping his eyes fixed on the dead child.

"Shotguns?" The ghost looked quizzically at Tom, then understanding dawned in his eyes. "Oh, yes, the fowling pieces. Those are curious. I didn't think they would do anything. There was one man who tried to shoot me when I came for him, but it didn't amount to much. But your friends, their pieces are different."

Tom reached the bed, and the person in the hall arrived at the door.

Whoever it was tried the doorknob and distracted the ghost long enough for Tom to drop down onto the carpet. A quick glance showed the underside of the bed to be filthy and cluttered.

And somewhere within it was the boarding pass.

"What are you doing?" the dead boy asked curiously.

"Wondering why this man didn't clean anything," Tom lied.

"Because he was a pig," the boy replied.

"Tom!" Victor called through the door.

"Is that your father?" the dead child asked.

Tom nodded.

"Good," the ghost said, grinning. "He can come with us."

The boy vanished, and Tom dove into the mess under the bed.

CHAPTER 47:
A RETURN TO CONSCIOUSNESS

Sara awoke with pain in her head and right shoulder. Her stomach churned with the intensity of her injuries, and she got to her feet carefully.

I have to focus, she thought, putting one hand against the cold wall to steady herself.

"Tom?!" Victor yelled, panic in his voice.

Sara heard the rattle of a doorknob, and she knew Tom Daniels was in danger.

With legs that were weak and wobbly, she climbed the stairs.

"Victor," Ariana hissed, and then a shotgun went off.

Sara reached the second-floor hallway, and her eyes instantly took in the situation.

Ariana was propped against the back wall across from the stairs, her shotgun in her hand as she fumbled to reload it. Victor was crumpled against a door at the far end of the hallway.

And the dead boy stood between them, a pleased smile on his face.

"When we're all done," he said, looking from Sara to Ariana, "I am going to drown all four of you in the bathtub, just like kittens. Won't that be fun?"

Ariana's response was to pull the trigger, and the boy vanished.

"Are you alright?" Sara asked, limping to the other woman.

"Nope," Ariana hissed, shaking her head. "Couple of ribs are busted. I can't move. Not yet. Tom's in the room at the end of the hall. Victor's—"

"Here," the man said groggily. "Here."

Victor straightened up and reached for the doorknob.

And the dead boy appeared behind him.

"My father never cared this much," the child said, and Sara winced as Ariana's shotgun misfired.

The boy looked over his shoulder, grabbed the back of Victor's head and drove the man's face into the door, causing it to shudder in the frame.

Victor slid down to lay limply on the floor.

"You are all boring," the ghost said, skipping a few steps toward them. "Bang, bang, bang. That's all you do. You shoot me. You punch me. But I keep coming back. I'm dead. I can't be dead again. The only one of you who is interesting is Tom. I like Tom. He's going to be my friend. He'll ride up top with me in the wheelhouse when we go back on the *Lady Elgin*."

The dead boy stopped several feet in front of them and asked, "What do you think of that?"

"I think," Ariana said in a low, pained voice, "that you should be drowned again."

Anger filled the child's face, and he pointed a shaking finger at her. "You're going to drown. And then, I'll bring you back, and I'll drown *you* again!"

"Sounds good to me," Ariana whispered. "Just do me a favor and shut up. You're annoying as hell."

The boy screamed with rage and took a step forward. "I am going to kill you forever."

Sara interjected herself between the dead child and Ariana and instantly regretted it.

Almost as an after-thought, the boy grabbed Sara with hands colder than anything she had felt before. Sneering, he half-turned and threw her down the hall and into a door. The cheap wood cracked beneath the impact and Sara fell into a bathroom.

Terror swelled within her and she grabbed hold of the edge of the filthy tub, trying to pull herself into a standing position.

A second later Ariana was thrown into the bathroom as well,

smashing into the sink and sagging to her knees. Sara heard the terrible wheeze the other woman's lungs made as she struggled to breathe, and once more Sara understood that the dead boy would kill them both.

The child appeared in the doorway, smirking.

"There is nowhere for you to go now," he said, stepping into the room.

Ariana tried to stand, and he threw her into the bathtub.

"Stop," Sara begged.

"No," he replied, and pushed her into the tub on top of Ariana.

The hateful squeak of a faucet rang out and a moment later water poured forth from the bathtub's faucet.

Panic drove Sara to her feet and she swung clumsily at the boy.

He ducked the blow easily, laughed, and then shoved her back into the tub.

"You're weak," the boy said, keeping Sara in the tub without any difficulty. "And I am going to enjoy this. We will play all night. Again and again. And when you are too tired, well, I will get the father and the son in here, and they will play, too."

The dead boy grinned and asked, "Doesn't that sound wonderful?"

"You shutting up sounds wonderful," Ariana muttered, the sound of her voice taking her by surprise.

"I mean," Ariana continued, "if we're being perfectly honest here. You're a whiny little brat. You sound like a pig, did you know that? All I here when you talk is, oink, oink, oink!"

The boy screamed, and Sara clapped her hands over her ears as the room reverberated with the sound.

He stepped forward, pushed Sara aside and reached for Ariana's head.

"Here we go," Ariana whispered with a weak grin. "The most spoiled child in the history of children is going to have another tantrum."

Pure hatred filled the dead boy's eyes, then he stiffened, twisted around, and yelled out, "No!"

***

When Tom's hands fell on the boarding pass the cold bit into his fingers.

With a gasp of pain, Tom jerked his hand back and shook open the lead-lined bag. Grimacing, he picked up the boarding pass as the dead boy yelled from the hallway.

Too bad, Tom thought, *you murderous little psychopath.*

And he stuffed the item into the bag and closed it with a twist.

Warmth rushed into the room and Tom dropped his head to the floor in relief, exhaustion, and fear for his father.

CHAPTER 48

SAFE AND AT HOME

Tom's snores could be heard in the kitchen, and the sound made Victor smile. His lower back continued to ache, despite the fact that it had been three days since Tom had saved them all.

"What's the smile about?" Sara asked before she took another bite of steak.

"My boy," Victor replied. "It's good to hear him."

The detective nodded, chewed her food, and then asked, "Have you heard from Ariana?"

"This morning," Victor answered. "Tom and I will be traveling up to see her tomorrow. She's going to look at the information we took from Korzh. She's hoping we might be able to track him down, get a jump on him."

"You shouldn't tell me any more," Sara said. "I don't want to know about a possible crime."

Victor nodded.

"And after you see her," Sara said after a moment. "What will you do?"

"I thought we might take a trip," Victor answered. He looked at the lead-lined bag that rested between them. "We may go up to Nashua. Stop in and see our friend Shane. I'm hoping he'll be able to help us with this ghost."

"Nashua's not that far from Concord," Sara said. "Think you might want to come on up for a visit? I don't get much company."

"I'd be happy to," Victor replied. "I know Tom will be, too. We've enjoyed your company the past few days."

"Especially since we're all alive," Sara said. "Do you think Shane will be able to help you get some place to destroy the boarding pass?"

"I hope so," Victor said. "I don't want to do it alone, but I don't want Tom with me either. If something were to go wrong—well, I wouldn't be able to deal with Tom being hurt because of it."

"I understand," Sara said. The woman glanced at her watch. "I need to go in a few minutes if I'm to get back to the hotel at a decent time."

"Do you want a cup of tea before you go?" he asked.

"Yes," Sara said, smiling. "That would be nice."

Victor stood up, cleared the dishes and started the teapot. Tom's snores continued to ring out from the bedroom, and the sun began its slow descent.

***

A vibrancy had returned to the neighborhood, despite the number of people who had mysteriously died. Sara could hear the songs of night-birds, and she saw the occasional deft swoop of a bat as she pulled her rental car to a stop in front of Nancy's house.

With the car still running, Sara looked at the building, gripped the steering wheel and finally managed to turn the engine off.

She climbed out of the car, jingling the keys nervously in one hand. Walking up the narrow, grass-choked walkway, Sara felt the rising sense of panic within her.

Death had nearly claimed her in Nancy's house, and the memory of the imminent drowning was forceful.

But the unknown child was trapped, and Sara needed to go in.

She had to.

When she let herself into the house, she met the same, tall ghost who had warned her before.

"You're back," the man said in a surprised but pleased voice.

"I am," Sara answered, refusing to close the door behind her.

"Excellent," he said. "You caught the little monster?"

She nodded.

The dead man frowned and asked, "Then why aren't we free?"

"That's why I'm here," Sara explained. "To let you know that it should be soon. We have to destroy the boarding pass, and it needs to be done far away."

For a moment, it looked as though the man might question her, then he shrugged and said, "Fine. No reason for me to be upset. I'm already dead."

A chill wafted down the stairs, and Sara glanced up.

"Don't go there," the man said in a gentle voice. "If you tell them what you told me, why, it would only upset them. I know the ones who understand that we're dead. I will speak to them. The others can wait. This is all a dream. Some good, some bad. We'll let them make their own determinations on that, alright?"

Sara turned her attention back to the old man and nodded.

"Alright," she said.

"Go home, get some shut-eye," the dead man said, grinning. "You look just about done in."

"I feel it," Sara said, and then stifled a yawn.

"Yes," the old man said, fading as he spoke. "Go and sleep. You've done well."

Sara waited only a moment after he disappeared before she turned and left the house, closing the door gently behind her. In a few minutes, she was backing her car into a parking space at the hotel and wondering if she would be able to sleep at all before her flight home.

CHAPTER 49

BEYOND THEIR UNDERSTANDING

Stefan slipped on his loafers, adjusted his belt, and smiled at himself in the mirror.

He looked exactly as he had intended; as another member of the suburban population. A father who was a mid-level executive in an accounting firm. He picked up a weathered and faded brown-leather wallet and flipped through it. There were pictures of two kids in soccer uniforms. He had his imaginary family's backstory memorized, and he even had a couple of business cards for a small firm in Boston. Stefan paid the owner a small amount to keep his false identity on the books as an employee.

It worked out for the best. The owner had Stefan's salary on the accounts, but all of the money went back into the man's own pockets.

And he knows, Stefan thought, adjusting the collar of his salmon-colored polo shirt, *that I'll gut him and let him bleed out if he backstabs me.*

Stefan picked up a wig, added a small amount of adhesive to the interior, and slipped it onto his head. He corrected the placement, then picked up a hand mirror so he could see the back of the wig as well.

The hairpiece was not flattering. It was a light brown with gray mixed in, and it gave the impression of standard, male-pattern baldness.

Satisfied that he looked as dull as possible, Stefan left the room. He glanced out the window and saw the unmarked police vehicle up the street.

They were watching him, to make certain he didn't leave without their knowledge while they looked for a way to link him to Officer

Colette's murder.

Too bad they found the body parts so soon, Stefan thought, sighing. He picked up his eye patch, put it in his pocket and put on a pair of sunglasses.

The police knew he only had one car and so they were focused on that.

But this man, Stefan thought, walking into the kitchen and opening a cabinet. *Mr. Jon Dinsmore, CPA for Long and Sons out of Boston, Massachusetts, well, he has a car as well.*

Stefan took down a pair of keys, one for a deadbolt and the other for a Master Lock and left his house by the back door. He walked to the side of his garage, entered through a small door, then exited through the back.

Quick steps carried him to a small path that ran between the fences of the houses behind him, and he maneuvered through the warren of tall grass, discarded bottles, and tight corridors as he moved farther from his safe house.

When Stefan stepped out onto the sidewalk several streets away, he whistled and stuffed his hands into the pockets of his beige slacks. He allowed himself a slow and steady gait as he traveled to his destination, a warehouse tucked into the end of a street. The building was divided into units and was truly nothing more than a glorified storage facility.

Stefan rented a small space, under the name of Jon Dinsmore, and he kept some necessities in it.

He used his key to unlock the deadbolt of the battered steel door and flicked on the lights as he entered. A tall, military surplus wall-locker stood against the wall behind a dark green, Volvo station-wagon.

Going to the locker, Stefan used the other key on the Master Lock and opened the doors. He removed the key to the Volvo as well as a small, .38 caliber pistol. Like the car, the weapon was legally registered to Jon Dinsmore, and Stefan even had a concealed carry permit.

Finally, he took out a new phone and turned it on.

Smiling, Stefan closed the locker, secured it again, and walked to the roll-up garage door that would allow him to drive the car out. Stefan punched in the four-digit passcode and waited for the door to rattle and roll up towards the ceiling on its tracks.

Looking out at the street beyond, Stefan's smile widened into a grin.

Time to go back to Fox Cat Hollow, he thought, getting into his car. *And kill Victor and Tom Daniels.*

Humming, Stefan eased the Volvo out into the morning.

CHAPTER 50:
A FURNISHED APARTMENT

Ariana sat propped up on the couch, a bag of ice held against her broken ribs and a bottle of Advil on the table beside her. Against her doctor's orders, there was a new bottle of vodka alongside the medicine.

Tom and Victor sat in a pair of over-stuffed easy chairs, and the teen was adjusting the straps on his prosthetic.

The two of them had arrived early in the morning, and they had spent most of the day with her, making sure she had everything she needed. She didn't have the heart to tell them that she was more than capable of looking after herself, or that she enjoyed their company.

Ariana had spent the majority of her life being self-sufficient, and she was embarrassed to find that she was pleased with Victor and Tom's consideration.

"Have you heard back from Shane Ryan?" she asked.

Victor shook his head. "I left a voicemail, and I sent him a text message. I figure he'll get back to me when he can."

"Make sure you put the boarding pass in something a little more durable than your bag," Ariana said. "The last thing you need is for that little sailor to get out and try to shanghai you."

Tom snorted out a chuckle, and Ariana winked at him.

"Agreed," Victor said. "What are you going to do?"

"For now," she said, wincing as she adjusted her position on the couch, "I'm going to heal up. If you want to leave the thumb-drive with me, I'll see what I can get off it. Then we can hunt down my half-brother and have a little chat."

"Sounds good to me," Tom said.

"You've got a little bit of bloodlust," Ariana said.

"A lot," Tom corrected.

She nodded and looked from the man to the child and smiled. "I shouldn't be out of action for too long. In fact, I'll probably start looking through the information on the drive as soon as you guys go. Just do me a favor."

"What's that?" Victor asked.

"Don't go after him on your own," she said. "And don't go back to the warehouse."

"Why not the warehouse?" Tom asked.

"Anne Le Morte," Ariana answered. "Best case scenario, she's still out there, trying to get someone to be her new caretaker."

"And worst case?" Victor asked in a soft voice.

"She's looking for us," Ariana answered, and silence filled the room.

***

Behind him, the scouts grumbled and complained, and Mark Richards bit his tongue.

They all need this damned badge, he thought, guiding them along the trail. *Like I want to be out here when it's humid, and the mosquitos think I'm the best dish on the buffet.*

"Mr. Richards," Mel Centage said.

Mark rolled his eyes, forced a smile onto his face and glanced over his shoulder. "What is it, Mel?"

"Do you hear singing?" the chubby boy asked.

Mark started to say no, then stopped.

He did hear singing.

A beautiful voice sang out loud and clear.

Mark knew he should leave the singer in peace, but he had to see who it was. He had never heard such a beautiful sound produced by a person before.

Without waiting to see if the scouts were following him, Mark turned off onto a smaller trail and moved towards the song.

Behind him, the boys complained and hastened to keep up.

Within a minute, they became silent, focused on the singer as well.

Mark soon stepped out into a small clearing where a tent was pitched off to the left. The remains of a campfire lay dull and black within a circle of soot marked stones, and a pile of broken and burnt bones lay off to one side. Trash littered the ground, but not near the opening to the tent.

Mark approached it with heavy feet, his eyes focused on the tent, his mind determined to see the singer.

As he reached the tent, Mark peered in.

He couldn't see anyone, but the singing stopped, and a woman spoke to him in French.

It was an archaic form, nothing like the French he had learned from the sisters at Holy Trinity School. But Mark grasped what the woman said.

"Pick it up," she said, her voice sweet. "Will you do this, for me?"

He nodded dumbly, bent down, and picked it up.

Mark turned around to face the boys.

Mel Centage blinked and asked, "What's that for?"

The shotgun roared, and the boys began to scream.

CHAPTER 51

NO TRUST

"She's dangerous," Carl said in German.

"I know, Carl," Shane sighed, replying in the same. He lit a fresh cigarette and shook his head. "I can tell she's dangerous. I'm just deciding what I should do with her."

"She is an old woman," Carl began.

Shane shook his head. "We know what people can do, regardless of age or gender."

It was Carl's turn to sigh, and the dead man did just that. "Then what do you suggest?"

Shane rubbed at the back of his head, tracing old scars with his fingers. "You know what, she's had enough time to cool her heels. I'm going to grab a shot or two of whiskey, maybe smoke a few more cigarettes. Then, we'll meet back here, and we'll have a little chat with her."

"Why not allow me and perhaps one of the others to escort her out of the house?" Carl's voice had a note of hope.

Shane shook his head. "She'll only come back if she really needs what she's after. And to be honest, it seems like she really needs what she's after. Best to finish it."

When the dead German didn't say anything, Shane nodded and walked toward the kitchen.

"My young friend," Carl called out.

"What?" Shane asked over his shoulder.

"How much whiskey?"

"One or two shots," Shane answered.

"Tomorrow then?" Carl asked.

Shane's laughter filled the hall and he replied, "Yeah. Tomorrow then."

***

Leanne had been in the room for days.

Bread and water had been left for her, but nothing else.

The door could not be forced, nor could the windows. She had not bothered wasting her energy on trying to break out.

Her stomach grumbled and her mouth salivated at the thought of fresh meat, and Leanne felt as though she was descending into madness.

None of that, she chided herself. *He'll show up eventually. Why else would he feed me?*

But there was a nagging sense of doubt.

She wondered if the dead hadn't tricked her into coming into the house. If they hadn't known what she was after.

Leanne pushed the thoughts away.

Calm, she thought. *I will remain calm, and I will seize my moment when it comes.*

A key rattled in the door lock, and Leanne smiled.

And it looks like that moment is now.

She straightened up and waited for the door to open.

***

Stefan Korzh stood in Victor Daniels' kitchen and sighed.

No one was home.

There wasn't any sign of where they had gone to.

He had been through the entirety of the small house, and not only were they not home, but there wasn't even anything interesting to steal or destroy.

Stefan stood in the basement, near a rough and poorly equipped station set up to load shotgun shells and work on weapons. The sawed-off lengths of a shotgun's barrel lay on the floor; the hacksaw it was done with on the workbench.

As Stefan turned to go back to the first floor, something caught his eye.

A small bag lay on a shelf, half in shadow beneath the bench. It seemed as though it had been shoved in hastily, and without much worry as to its discovery.

Stefan leaned over, reached out to pick it up and waves of cold emanated from it. After a moment's pause, he plucked it off the shelf and felt the weight of the fabric, which was far more than it should have been.

Cold and heavy, Stefan thought, grinning. *Is this one of my family's items? Something I let loose into the world?*

And it's come back to me?

Stefan chuckled and tried to think what he might have recently sent out.

Oh, he thought, laughing. *You're from the Lady Elgin. All those dry-land drownings. Well, I think you'll come home with me. Maybe we can drop you off somewhere else, hm?*

Still holding the bag, Stefan left the basement and reached the kitchen with a smile on his face. As he considered the bag in his hands, he heard a pair of voices. Male and female.

"Matt," the young woman said on the other side of the door. "You are such a brat."

"Hey," Matt replied. "That's what big brothers are for."

He drew his .38 and waited.

The deadbolt was unlocked, and the back door swung open, revealing a young woman and a young man.

They froze, surprised at the sight of Stefan.

"Hello," Stefan said, and he shot each of them in the chest.

They collapsed against one another as they fell, and Stefan stepped over them as he left the house. He paused once and shot each in the head.

No witnesses, he thought, heading for the path that would take him to the back of the Fox Cat Hollow library. *No witnesses ever.*

Humming, Stefan holstered his weapon and tossed the bag from one hand to the other as he vanished into the woods.

* * *

AT THE ESTATE SALE

Felix hated yard sales, estate sales, flea markets, and everything else that had the potential to require haggling. He knew it was a tried-and-true past-time of the New Englander. But he wasn't a New Englander, at least not by birth; and the fact that Melissa seemed to thrive on negotiating the price of *everything* left him questioning his life choices.

But Melissa was seven months pregnant, and he would rather be disgruntled in silence than harass her about antiquing.

"What do you think of this?" she asked, interrupting his train of thought.

"Hm?" Felix looked at what she held in her hands and saw it was a silver baby's rattle. He hated it. Smiling, he said, "I think it looks great. Do you like it?"

"I love it," she replied, dropping her free hand to her extended belly and rubbing it absently. "I think she will, too."

"I'm sure she will," Felix said, and he turned away to look for the sports memorabilia that had been advertised. Behind him, Felix heard Melissa begin her negotiations. He rolled his eyes and wandered out of the room. Other people pressed against him, and no one, not a single individual, excused themselves. Each was focused on some unknown goal.

It's like they're robbing the dead in here, he thought, stepping into a small study. The room appeared to have been struck by a tornado. Papers littered the floor and desk, books lay on their sides and stacked haphazardly on the study's shelves. He could smell old pipe tobacco, and the room was stifling. Sunlight streamed in through a dirty window, and Felix wondered how long it had been since someone had bothered to clean the house.

Probably before I was born, he thought with a dry chuckle.

He poked around for a few minutes in the study, then with a shrug, he exited the room and went to find Melissa.

She smiled and waved at him while a bored teenager wrapped the silver rattle in a piece of newspaper.

"Anything?" she asked when he came to a stop beside her.

"No," he answered.

"I'm sorry."

"That's okay," Felix said. "Do you want to stop and get a hot chocolate and a donut on the way home?"

Melissa's eyes lit up, and she nodded.

She had been a compulsive coffee drinker before the start of the pregnancy, and she had been forced to switch to hot chocolate because of the caffeine in the coffee. Melissa drank at least three cups of hot chocolate a day, sometimes more if she was feeling particularly bad. Both he and the doctor had warned her about gestational diabetes, but Melissa didn't care about it.

And Felix knew that he shouldn't give her more sugar, but he didn't want to listen to her complain either.

"Here," the teenager said, handing the bag to Melissa.

"I've got it," Felix said, accepting it from the teen.

Melissa beamed at him, and they left the house together.

Felix shifted the bag from one hand to the other, wondering why it had suddenly grown colder.

***

Felix yawned and deleted his browser history before he turned off his laptop. Leaning back against the couch, he glanced at the silver rattle, then he picked it up and held it up to the light. A pair of initials and a date, *E.S. 1915,* were engraved under the ball-shaped top, and Felix wondered how much the silver might be worth. He had hoped to find a maker's mark on the item, some clue that would allow him to research it a little more.

Felix didn't think it would be worth enough to get them out of the Hesser Apartment complex, but it was nice to dream.

Sighing, he returned it to the table and rubbed his hands together. The silver felt abnormally cold, and it irritated him when he held it.

He had the feeling someone was watching him whenever he did so.

Felix stood up, went into the kitchen and opened the cabinet over the refrigerator. He moved aside several cookbooks, reached back and felt around for the pint of whiskey he kept hidden there.

Melissa had banned all alcohol from the house the day she had found she was pregnant. And in theory, but not practice, Felix had agreed with her. He had agreed with her reasoning that they needed to stop acting like they were teenagers, and he had helped her pour all the liquor out.

Then he had stopped at the package store and purchased himself a pint.

He wasn't acting like a teen, he just liked to have a drink now and again.

Felix didn't bother getting out a glass. Instead, he unscrewed the top and drank right from the bottle. When he had his fill, he put the cap back on, returned everything to the way it had been, and walked back to the sofa. Easing himself down, he glanced at the rattle.

That's not right, he thought, frowning. *It should be there.*

The rattle was gone.

Felix slid off the couch, got on his hands and knees and peered under the table.

The rattle was there.

He reached out, then jerked his hand back, surprised at how painfully cold the small item was.

What the hell? he thought, pushing himself into a sitting position.

His brain moved sluggishly, wading through the whiskey as he tried to figure out what to do.

He turned around and stopped, surprised.

A young woman stood a few feet away from him. Her face was slightly round, her cheeks plump. The girl's hair was gathered into a bun at the nape of her neck, and she wore what looked like a maid's outfit, similar to those worn on the BBC shows Melissa made him watch.

"Are you the child's father?" the young woman asked in a thick, Irish brogue.

"How the hell did you get in here?" he demanded, getting to his feet.

"Father or not," she said, "the babe doesn't need the likes of you. No child needs a father. You teach them nothing but bad things."

"You better leave," Felix said, taking a step towards her. "I'm going to call the cops."

She frowned and looked up at him. "You'd be a terrible influence."

"Right," Felix said, reaching out for her arm. But his hand passed through her, and he jerked it back, his skin feeling as though he had soaked it in ice for an hour.

"What the hell?" he asked, stepping away.

The back of his knee hit the coffee table, and he fell over it, crashing to the floor. As he tried to get up, she sprang onto him. Her left hand pried his mouth open, and she whispered, "Terrible influence."

She drove her hand into his mouth, and he screamed. The pain was beyond anything he had experienced before.

He could feel her cold fingers wriggling down into his throat, digging into parts of his body that he hadn't known existed. Felix let out another, desperate shriek as her fingers wrapped around his innards and began to pull.

His screams became muffled as the first of his intestines were yanked out of his mouth.

THE INFORMATION HIGHWAY

The ringing of the phone was a welcome distraction from work, and Victor Daniels answered it happily.

"Mr. Daniels," James Moran said. "How are you, sir?"

"I'm doing well, thank you," Victor replied, relaxing into his chair. "This is an unexpected pleasure."

"I'm glad to hear that," the other man said. "Unfortunately, it is not with pleasant news that I'm reaching out to you."

"What's wrong?" Victor asked.

"I seem to have a problem," James stated. "You see, when Jeremy Rhinehart was still alive, well, he was the man to whom I would go with my concerns and issues. I was hoping I might do the same with you."

"I don't know how qualified I am to assist you," Victor said. "But I'm honored that you think I am."

"Oh, don't sell yourself short, Mr. Daniels," the other man said. "You've done remarkably well for an individual thrust into a world few people know of, let alone survive."

"Alright," Victor said, grinning, "tell me what it is you need help with."

"An item has appeared in Massachusetts. In the town of Groton, to be precise," James said. "Do you know of the place?"

"I do," Victor said, painful memories of Erin flashing before him. "What's this item?"

"A silver rattle. For a baby," James said.

Victor leaned forward, took a pad of paper off his desk, and jotted down the information. "And what does this particular item do?"

James cleared his throat, then said, "Do you have access to the dark web, Mr. Daniels?"

"I do," Victor answered.

"Then my suggestion would be to access it and search for Groton and Felix Ulster," James said.

Victor added the name to his notes. "And who is Felix Ulster?"

"The victim, I am afraid. And," James added, "unless you have a strong stomach, I would avoid searching for any photographs of the crime scene."

"Alright," Victor said. "I'll do what I can."

"As an aside, Mr. Daniels," James continued. "I would leave young Tom home."

"He's off camping with his girlfriend and her family for the weekend," Victor said. "But I thank you for the advice."

They said goodbye and Victor ended the call. He pulled his chair closer to the desk, accessed the dark web, and did as James Moran had suggested.

But when the crime scene photos were accessible, Victor looked at them.

Felix Ulster had been a pudgy 29-year-old who had been living with his pregnant girlfriend. She had been the one to discover the body, and the sight of the corpse had sent her into premature labor. According to the police report, she remained hospitalized. The labor had been stopped, but she couldn't be moved.

Felix, Victor saw, had died on the couples' couch, and he had not died well.

The man's intestines had been pulled from his body and strung about the room. They hung from the ceiling fan and were draped along the back of the couch.

The most disturbing aspect of the scene wasn't the intestines, but the fact that whoever had done the crime had managed to do so by pulling the organ out of the man's mouth.

There was no incision in the stomach.

The medical examiner listed death as a combination of shock and suffocation.

Unwillingly, Victor went back to the crime scene photos and clicked on them, enlarging them and poring over each.

Then a bit of silver caught his eye, and a grim smile spread across his face.

Beneath the coffee table, tucked into a shadow, was a small, silver rattle.

Victor returned to the police report, searched through it and found confirmation that Felix's girlfriend, Melissa Landry, wasn't expected to be released from Lowell Hospital for at least another week.

Victor wrote down the address of the couple, shut his computer down and went to pack.

He would leave as soon as he was ready.

Victor paused when he reached the doorway to his room, gripping the doorframe tightly. His body still ached from the recent events in Connecticut. The struggle against the ghost of the old woman had been brutal and although it had been days since the encounter, Victor felt it might be several more before his body healed entirely.

Why do I keep doing this? he thought. But as soon as the question arrived, it was answered.

Because of Erin, Victor thought, the memory of his wife leaping to the forefront of his thoughts. *Everything is for her.*

Sadness swept over him and Victor swallowed the lump that had risen in his throat. With his thumb he wiped away the few tears that escaped and let out a long, mournful sigh.

Well, I know I won't be able to sleep tonight, he thought, going into his room. *Not at all.*

The memory of his wife flickered and vanished, replaced by the vicious images of the crime scene.

FRUSTRATION AND ANNOYANCE

Gary Corriveau was half-asleep in his chair when Shannon walked in.

"You okay?" she asked.

He shook his head. "Feel like garbage."

She gave him an understanding smile. "Well, she's asleep."

Gary managed a weak grin. "Good. She was up most of the night."

"So were you," his wife said, coming forward and giving him a kiss. "Thank you for staying up with her."

"Hey," he said, "you have a presentation this morning. I don't. I have plenty of sick time, and work can just deal with it."

"They love you," she said, laughing. Then she winked and said, "I love you."

"Love you, too, babe," Gary said. "She still asleep?"

Shannon nodded, adding, "Make sure you turn on the monitor before you pass out, okay?"

"You got it," he said, and he waved as his wife left for work.

Gary listened to the tumblers fall into place as she locked the door and he picked up the baby-monitor from the side-table. He turned it on, raised the volume, and smiled at the sweet sound of Sonia's delicate snores.

Gary returned the monitor to the table, extended the footrest of his chair, and wished he could go and lie down in his own bed.

That would be a mistake, he thought, closing his eyes. Even if he brought the monitor, the comfort of his bed would make getting up almost impossible to achieve. Better to rest fitfully than risk not hearing his two-year-old.

Gary yawned again, crossed his arms over his chest and let his head sag to the right. Around him, the apartment building went through its morning ritual, and the familiarity of those sounds helped lull him to sleep.

The sound of singing woke Gary up, and he blinked, not quite sure if he had dreamed it or not.

But the red light on the baby-monitor fluttered and flickered, the song soft as it wavered. He listened for a moment, then smiled.

Probably getting interference from something, he thought, closing his eyes again.

"Yes," a woman said in a gentle voice, "you're a sweet girl. Look at that red hair of yours. Why it's piled right on, isn't it?"

Gary straightened up, his heart thundering in his chest.

Sonia had deep, red hair.

He launched himself out of the chair, stumbling as he fought for his balance, bouncing off the wall as he turned down the hallway. In a few steps, he reached Sonia's nursery and came to a stop.

His daughter lay on her back, sleeping.

But by the crib stood a short woman, the morning sun passing through her as if she were nothing more than a piece of dark gauze hung over the window.

Shock swept over him, but fear for his daughter's safety propelled him into the room.

The creature that stood beside the crib turned around and faced him, and Gary saw that it had the face of a young, teenage girl. She wore an old maid's uniform, and her face had a serious expression on it.

"Are you the child's father?" she asked.

Gary's mouth worked for a moment before he could answer her. "Yes."

"A child doesn't need a father," the woman said stiffly, tilting her head up disdainfully.

"You need to leave," Gary said. His mind tried to grasp the flimsy nature of the creature before him, and all he could drag up from the depths of his sleep-deprived mind was a vague memory of a vampire movie he had watched as a teenager. "You can't be in my house. I didn't give you permission to be here."

"Are you daft, man?" the stranger asked incredulously. "What in goodness' name do you think I am?"

"You're a vampire," he stuttered. "You need to get away from my daughter."

The young woman let out a surprised and pleasant laugh as she shook her head. "No, you great idiot. I'm dead, not undead."

Gary frowned, not sure what to say.

"My name is Bridget O'Faolain," she said. "And I'm a ghost. And you, you foul thing, you're the worst beast a child could meet. A father."

"What?" Gary asked, shaking his head.

"I've seen what fathers do," Bridget said, her voice becoming low and cold. "I've *felt* them."

A dark, brutal fear washed over Gary, and he shivered.

"You need to leave my little girl alone," he said, his voice shaking. "You get away from her. Do you understand me?"

"I won't hurt her," Bridget said, taking a small step towards him. "You needn't worry about that."

"Then leave," Gary said, forcing himself to stand his ground. *She can't hurt me. She's just a ghost. There's nothing she can do to me.*

"I'll leave soon enough," Bridget said. "But not until I've taught you a lesson."

She reached out and grabbed his upper arm, and Gary bit back a scream as a shooting pain exploded through the muscle. His eyes flickered to Sonia, and when he looked again at Bridget, there was an expression of pure malice on her face.

"Come," she whispered, "let's not wake the child."

Before he could respond, Gary was jerked off his feet. Bridget dragged him out of the room and down the hall, and he struggled the entire way. Nothing he did freed him from her grasp, and she never slowed.

When they entered the family room, the ghost hurled him across it, and he smashed into his chair, knocking it over. He rolled over it and slammed into the wall. Adrenaline pumped through him as he tried to get to his feet, but Bridget was there.

She slapped him across the face with enough force to send him to the floor in a heap. Stars exploded around his eyes, and his ears rang. He tried to pull away as she grabbed him by his arms and flipped him onto his back.

The ringing lessened in his ears as she leaned over him, a grim smile on her face.

"In my father's house," she said in a low voice, "I was a maid. I was his illegitimate child, and it was the desire of his wife that I be employed by him. So his sin might ever be before him. When he finally decided that he had had quite enough of the lot of us, he ground up glass and fed it to his wife and my mother, and his daughters, legitimate and otherwise. Do you know what glass feels like, in your stomach?"

Gary could only shake his head.

"It feels," she whispered, moving her face closer to his, "as if someone took your stomach and ripped it out through your mouth."

Bridget shoved her fist down his throat, and the baby-monitor came to life.

Sonia's cries echoed through the house, drowning out the muffled shrieks of her father.

THE RIGHT PLACE

Victor sat at a small café, an untouched bagel and a half-empty mug of coffee in front of him. Through the plate glass window, he was able to look at the old Victorian that had been turned into an apartment building, and at the police officers who had cordoned the property off. There were several State Troopers, and each member of law enforcement Victor saw wore an expression of disturbed concern.

"We normally don't have this much excitement." The barista had come out from behind the coffee bar and stood near the door, arms crossed over his thin chest.

"No?" Victor asked.

The young man shook his head, blonde hair flopping as he did so. "No. Police aren't saying what happened, but that's two deaths in the same building. And in two days. Kind of freaky."

"Is it a gas leak or something?" Victor asked, playing dumb.

"Don't think so," the barista said, stroking his goatee and then shrugging. "I mean, if it was, wouldn't the gas company be here? And besides, it was just the dad, at least that's what one of the regulars said. She heard the baby crying, and when she went over to the apartment to see if everything was alright, no one answered, and the baby kept on screaming. They finally called the police, and that was when they found the father dead."

"That's terrible," Victor said.

The young man nodded, then glanced at him, saw Victor hadn't touched his bagel and asked, "Everything okay with the food?"

"Yes," Victor answered, smiling. "I thought I was hungry, but it turned out I just needed a little more coffee."

"Ah," the barista said, nodding with understanding. "Gotcha."

He stood silently for several more minutes, seemed to grow bored with the drama across the street and returned to his position behind the bar.

I know why they're not saying anything, Victor thought, sipping his coffee. *Because people would lose their minds if they thought they could spontaneously vomit their intestines out.*

Victor settled into the chair and waited for the police to leave.

***

At 6:17 PM, the last of the police at the building left, and Victor had walked the better part of Groton, which wasn't a large town. He had explored the old cemeteries, visited the library, and eaten lunch and dinner at a small Chinese restaurant.

Victor had also had the opportunity to examine the back of the apartment building, and he had been pleased to see that the rear entrance could be accessed without a key.

Victor's phone rang suddenly, but it was a private number and he had no desire to speak with anyone.

Not now, he thought, putting the phone back down. *No distractions now.*

Victor reached into the back seat of his car and removed the lead-lined bag and his handmade lock picks. The tools were heavy in his hand. Not from any real weight, but rather from the knowledge that if he was caught with them, he would have a difficult time explaining why he had them.

In a building where two people had died gruesomely, he added.

Well, Victor thought, getting out of his car. *He who dares wins.*

With that motto in his forethoughts, Victor approached the rear of the apartment building with a long, purposeful stride. He knew that any sort of hesitation, any hint that he might not belong there, would catch someone's attention. And with people on edge, it meant an instant call to the police.

But he had done some research as well. He knew who the pregnant woman was. Who her boyfriend had been. Victor had also seen where a photograph of the couple had been on the dresser and should anyone question him when he came out of the apartment, he had a solid cover story.

Or so he hoped.

I'm getting the photograph for Melissa, he told himself. *She wants it at the hospital. I'm a friend of Felix. I was his history professor at the University of Massachusetts in Lowell.*

He knew it was a thin story, but Victor doubted if anyone knew much of anything about the couple, since they had only moved into the building a few months earlier.

But I need to get into the apartment first, he thought, entering the building.

He hurried up to the third floor, sweat gathering at the small of his back as his anxiety increased. There was a thrill of excitement, that guilty pleasure he couldn't rid himself of when he thought of opening a door closed to him.

And then he was there. Apartment 3A.

The crime scene tape had been removed, for as far as the police knew, no crime had been committed. In the report Victor had managed to read online, there was no evidence of a foreign object used to eviscerate the man via his mouth.

Felix had been murdered though.

Just not by anyone living.

The sounds of people talking and watching television drifted into the hallway as Victor leaned in close to the door. He slipped a pair of picks into the deadbolt and carefully maneuvered them until the lock clicked. Then, with his heart beating against his chest, Victor eased the picks into the doorknob's lock.

A moment later it too clicked, and Victor let himself into the apartment.

Cold air washed over him, and he knew the rattle was still there.

He closed the door gently and locked it behind him. Quietly, he crossed the main room, stepping over bloodstains on his way to a tall window that looked out over the back of the building.

Victor unlocked the window's catch and slid the sash up. The gentle noises of Groton rolled into the room, and Victor opened the screen as well.

He looked at the fire escape, saw that it seemed to be in good condition, and hoped that would be the case if he needed it.

Twisting his iron ring around his finger nervously, Victor took a deep breath, removed his white cotton gloves from his pockets, and pulled them on.

It was time to retrieve the rattle.

Victor opened the lead-lined bag, turned around and almost dropped it to the floor.

The ghost stood before him, her hands clasped behind her back. Her head was tilted to one side as she looked at him. Then, with an air of resignation, she reached up and adjusted the small-cap she wore and asked, "Who are you?"

"My name's Victor, miss," he replied.

Her mouth twitched with humor.

"Miss, is it?" she asked, and he heard an Irish accent.

Victor wracked his brain, for when he was younger, he had attempted to learn Gaelic and failed for the most part. But there were phrases and odd words he still remembered.

"Yes," he said, then, in halting Gaelic, he added, "And I this evening is pleasant."

She chuckled. "That was a fair try, and I appreciate it, I do. But goodness, you sound like a man choking on a mouthful of bones."

Victor blushed but smiled as well.

"I don't speak it," he apologized.

"You don't say?" the dead woman said. "Now, you who cannot speak the tongue of all decent folk, tell me, why are you here?"

"I've come to take you with me, miss," Victor said.

The humor vanished from her face.

"And where would you take me?" she demanded.

"Home with me," he explained. "My son and I live in Pennsylvania."

"Your son?" the dead woman inquired.

Victor nodded.

"Then you're a father?" she asked.

And the murders clicked.

Felix had been a father-to-be.

The second victim's child had been screaming, which is how they found him.

No one else had been touched. Only the fathers.

"I am," Victor said in resignation, clenching his hand into a fist.

"I've no use for fathers," the dead girl said in a low growl. "None at all."

"I'm sorry," Victor said.

"Not yet," she hissed, "but soon enough."

He stood his ground as she approached him, the temperature plummeting as she drew nearer. Victor's breath exploded out of his mouth in great white clouds, and she reached out a small hand towards his face.

And he struck her with his fist, the iron ring passing through her and snapping her out of the room and back into her rattle.

No sooner was she gone than Victor threw himself to the floor, eyes questing for the possessed item beneath the table. He reached for it, and she was there, her foot stomping down on his forearm.

Pain shot through him, and he bit back a groan, forcing his hand toward the rattle despite the excruciating agony it caused.

A cold hand reached down, snatched him by the hair and jerked his head back as he closed his fingers on the rattle.

"I will make you suffer," the dead girl whispered to him. "I will drag your belly out by inches, and you shall scream, my fine father."

Grinding his teeth together, Victor jerked his arm back and dragged his iron ring through her foot. Her howl of rage ended as soon as it began, and his head dropped down with the sudden disappearance of her hand.

Victor rolled onto his back, gasping for breath, his thoughts clouded by the pain in his arm. His right hand was numb, and he had to look down at it to make certain he still had the rattle. A pained grin spread across his face and vanished a moment later as the dead girl appeared at his side.

She didn't waste any words.

Instead, she kicked him in the right thigh, the toe of her boot passed through the muscle, and his entire leg spasmed. Victor tried to roll away, but she took him by the arm and jerked him back.

"I always thought cats were cruel creatures," the dead girl murmured, a sly smile appearing. "But now I see the joy in prolonging the kill. What say you, mouse?"

Victor swung the lead-lined bag through her arm and grimaced at the high-pitched shriek that escaped her lips. She staggered back, clutching her head, her eyes closed tight in pain, and Victor seized the moment.

He forced his numb right hand to open the bag, and as the dead girl focused on him once more, he stuffed the rattle into the opening.

The ghost reached him as he went to close it, and she kicked viciously at him. Each blow shook him, his entire body trembling as he fought to tighten the straps of the bag before she beat him to death.

Or before he became too weak to resist her.

She paused once, let out a triumphant laugh and asked, "What will you do when I string your guts around the room like so much garland?"

Victor didn't have the strength to speak.

But he had enough to close the lead-lined bag.

The dead woman vanished, and he was alone, on his back, in the middle of a stranger's apartment. He stared at the ceiling, listened to a car pass by with its music blaring, and he smiled.

I'm alive, he thought, still too battered to move. Victor managed to lift the bag a little, its weight comforting.

And you're in here, he thought. He lowered the bag to the floor and slowed his heart rate, allowing his body to recover. His right hand remained numb, although feeling seemed to be returning to it. Victor's right thigh was a knot of pain and had her foot been solid, he was certain she would have broken the bone.

As he lay on the floor, Victor listened for sounds that might hint at the imminent arrival of the police. Or of anyone, for that matter.

Only the sounds of banal normality reached his ears, and Victor smiled.

He remained where he was for a few more minutes, then he pushed himself into a sitting position, caught his breath, and got to his feet. Victor struggled to the door, unlocked it and opened a crack. He straightened up as best he could and stepped out into the hallway.

Victor didn't bother locking the door behind him.

It was more than enough to put one foot in front of the other and limp his way to the stairs, the lead-lined bag clutched in his left hand, and pain replacing the numbness in his right.

He was alive, and that was more than some.

He managed a weak smile, and the dull haze of pain that wrapped itself around him blinded him to the small hole in the lead-lined bag.

A hole that widened with each step he took.

* * *

Check out these best-selling series from our talented authors:

GHOST STORIES

RON RIPLEY
BERKLEY STREET SERIES
MOVING IN SERIES
HAUNTED COLLECTION SERIES
DEATH HUNTER SERIES

IAN FORTEY
JIGSAW OF SOULS SERIES
CULT OF THE ENDLESS NIGHT SERIES

SUPERNATURAL SUSPENSE

A. I. NASSER
SLAUGHTER SERIES
SIN SERIES

DAVID LONGHORN
NIGHTMARE SERIES
ASYLUM SERIES

SARA CLANCY
THE BELL WITCH SERIES
BANSHEE SERIES

For a complete list of our new releases and best-selling horror books, visit ScareStreet.com or scan the QR code below!